A Harper's

HARPER'S

MASSACHUSETTS

CONSCIENTIA

PREPARATORY

Education

A HARPER'S EDUCATION

LYDIA KELLY

WorldMaker
Media

WorldMaker Media

P.O. Box 610383

Newton, MA 02461

www.worldmakermedia.com

First published by WorldMaker Media, a division of
TheNextBigWriter, LLC on XXX.

ISBN:978-0-9838934-7-9

DEDICATION

For my parents, because love, hard work, and
dedication are learned values.

PROLOGUE

"**M**iss?"

"Miss?"

"What?" Laila responded sharply.

"I need to ask you a few questions, if that's all right."

She looked around her dorm room at the well-made bed, the poster of Yo-Yo Ma that Tennille had above her dresser, and over on her side of the room, his picture in the heart frame. Tears blurred her vision. Where was he? He said he would be right back. "I don't think so." Maybe the officer didn't hear her. Perhaps she hadn't really said anything? Or, he simply chose to ignore her answer.

"I understand you knew the deceased."

"They have names," Laila said, irritated. She didn't want to answer any questions. Laila wished she could hide away somewhere and forget everything she had just seen.

"Most people find it easier to keep things less personal," the officer said quietly.

"Would you find it easier? What if it was someone you knew?" She finally looked up at the young police officer, directly into his sympathetic brown eyes. His radio squawked and he turned down the volume. "I know this is difficult. I promise I only have a few questions for you."

Laila took a deep breath and attempted to push the images out of her mind – blood, pale skin, sprawled bodies. Her own screams echoed through her head. She started shaking and felt the bile moving up from her stomach. She closed her eyes and hugged herself tight.

"Do you remember what time it was when you heard the shots?"

Laila shuddered and shook her head. "I don't know. Around nine I guess."

"Do you know what might have caused this to happen?"

Was he serious? He knew what had gone on at Harper's Prep. No one had seen this coming though. Three dead students in the span of two weeks.

Laila closed her eyes again. The last two weeks had felt like a dream. Everything else seemed so insignificant now. "Things at Harper's have been fucked up since I've been here." She almost never swore but why bother holding back?

The officer raised one eyebrow and gave her a moment to wipe away her tears.

"Was this related to the incident last week? Did they all know each other?"

Laila nodded her head. "Yes."

"Were they all friends, enemies?"

"At Harper's you don't really know," she mumbled. Her body started to shake again and she looked around, trying to find something to steady her, someone to help her. Sterling, she thought, as grief overcame her. Why did he leave her alone? Was he okay?

"I think we should leave this until tomorrow," the young officer said, catching her look and understanding she couldn't go on. "Get some rest. I'm sorry for the loss," he said, before turning and walking out the door.

She sobbed and wanted to run into his strong arms. The world had collapsed around them but in his arms she felt safe. She felt a familiar touch; she didn't feel afraid to cry.

CHAPTER ONE

Seven months earlier…

The bass from a jacked up stereo pounded through Laila's body. Her new roommate, Tennille, had dressed her up, dragged her to the party, and forced her onto the dance floor. "I'm not in San Francisco anymore," she whispered to herself, descending the stairs. A couple kissed passionately in a corner and a tall blonde guy with cargo pants and a t-shirt gulped down something in a red cup. Yup, definitely not her old school.

She looked around the crowded basement. The bottom floor of the Wellsworth Hall dormitories opened from the stairs into a large room where the students danced and socialized. Fat, gothic pillars spiraled up from the foundation. Long, dark hallways crept from the main room and disappeared back around the building. Students relaxed and chatted on expensive looking couches and chairs. Blue and gold banners hung from the ceiling and the walls, proudly displaying the school colors and crest. That crest. Laila had been studying it ever since she had received her acceptance letter from Harper's. A horse and lion standing erect on their hind legs at either side of a shield, a knight's helmet above them, and the word *consciencia* bannered below. Laila assumed the founding fathers of Harper's had designed such an intricate crest with the intention of instilling a sense of pride and honor in all those who were deemed worthy of wearing it. Needless to say, she felt she had a lot to live up to.

Laila knew the aristocratic elite of the United States counted on Harper's to educate their children and prepare them for college – mostly Ivy League Universities. When her parents had suggested she attend the school, Laila had almost choked.

"Let me tell you who's who," Tennille said, breaking her thoughts.

"That guy over there, the one with the leather jacket and black hair, that's Julian Polk, kind of the leader of the popular crowd. His parents own Polk Industries, one of the largest makers of plastics and tapes in the country. The blonde girl standing next to him is Kalyn Andretti, his sometimes girlfriend, soon to be fiancée unless he impregnates someone else before graduation. Her parents are also filthy rich."

"Wait," Laila stopped her, trying to grasp the concept without laughing. "Why is she his soon to be fiancée if she's only his sometimes girlfriend?"

Tennille smiled at her question. "Welcome to Harper's, girl, where old money means old tradition.

11

Kalyn's family and Julian's go way back. They aren't allowed to call it an arranged marriage, but that's essentially what it is."

"Are you serious?"

"Hmm, afraid so," Tennille said. "Pretty archaic, don't you think?"

Laila nodded in disbelief. Her friends back home were going to love the stories she would have for them. They had all warned her about going to an East Coast school, but even they couldn't have imagined arranged marriages.

"Okay, so who else is here?"

"That guy standing next to Julian, staring at you like you're a perfect piece of filet mignon, that's Chase Nichols."

Laila squirmed in discomfort as she caught Chase's eye. His tall, lanky figure was slouched at the shoulders and his eyes looked red and swollen even from across the room. He wore his chestnut hair slicked back and he ran his tongue over his pale lips as he stared at the two girls.

"Chase gets away with almost everything because his parents donate an obscene amount of money to the school every year. His mother is a Harding, one of the founding families of the school and supposedly descended from someone on the Mayflower. He has a massive sense of entitlement that stretches into the female population, although he usually ends up with Julian's left-overs.

"Now, on the other side of the spectrum," Tennille continued, taking Laila's hand and spinning her around, "are the ones you don't have to look out for. The kid sitting alone in the corner, the one with red hair, that's Randy. He's one of two seniors here on scholarship, which means he doesn't have many friends."

"Who's the other one?"

"That would be yours truly." Tennille smiled proudly. "Although, I've managed to stay under the radar for the past three years."

"And Randy hasn't?"

"He used to be really bothered by all the ridicule. During his freshman year they almost expelled him for fighting because Julian and Chase and all their friends wouldn't leave him alone. I guess he just didn't know how to deal with it."

"He doesn't look like the type of guy who would get into a fight."

"He might not have money like everyone else here, but he can hold his own, that's for sure. But I think he's calmed down now. Either he doesn't let it bother him as much or he's become better at suppressing his anger."

"Poor guy."

"Oh, don't even think about feeling sorry for him," Tennille said. "He hates that more than anything. Randy's the most down-to-earth person in the school. That's probably why we're such great friends. We tell each other everything."

Tennille didn't really have a censor when it came to her opinions. "And what about you? How do you survive?" Laila asked.

13

"Me? I'm a novelty at this school. Harper's administrators are always looking to impress the board with their recruits. I'm a music prodigy with the added bonus of being, how did they put it, 'culturally diverse.'" Tennille sure didn't lack in the confidence department and there was no reason that she should. Her long black hair flowed like one continuous wave down her back and dark, thick lashes fluttered around her large brown eyes. Laila would have killed for Tennille's flawless mocha colored skin, but as it was, she was stuck wearing SPF 50 on a daily basis.

"And there they are," Tennille pointed to the stairs. Three figures entered the room, the dark light of the basement shadowing their silhouettes. The music almost seemed coordinated for their entrance and nearly all of the girls threw them sideways glances.

The boy in front had dark hair and towered over the rest of the students. His eyes searched the crowd. Two blonde boys trailed him, their ashy hair picking up the colors of the strobe lights. The closer of the two had a wide grin on his face and deep dimples. His twin brother looked more somber, his eyes fixed calmly on the crowd.

"Who are they?" Laila yelled, only to have the song end as she shouted the last words. Two girls next to them snickered. A slow song started playing.

"Hands off the dark-haired one, he's mine," Tennille laughed and waved her hand in the air. The boy with the dark hair gave her a crooked smile and pushed his way through the crowd.

"You're finally here!"

"I told you I would be," he said in a deep voice as Tennille threw her arms around his neck to kiss him. It wasn't indecent or prolonged, but it made Laila blush. She had never shown any public displays of affection but she supposed that was because she never had a boyfriend for long enough to display much of anything. At her old Catholic school, boys were scarce.

"Tate, this is my new roommate, Laila."

Tate extended his hand. "Welcome to Harper's Preparatory," he said with a bow.

"Thank you," Laila smiled.

"And this is Alistair and Sterling," Tennille said, before returning her attention to Tate.

"Laila, what a beautiful name." The cheerier of the blonde twins took her hand and brought it gently to his lips. "I'm Alistair, the more handsome of the Pierce twins."

His brother rolled his eyes behind Alistair's back. Laila smiled at his dimples. "You two look identical to me," she admitted.

"Almost, but not quite," Alistair continued.

"How am I supposed to tell the difference?"

"Sterling's got the crazy eyes. I've got the dimples." Alistair glanced at a group of girls standing a few feet away. "If you'll excuse me…"

Laila watched him leave, impressed by his confidence and ease. She turned back to his brother, a

15

little disappointed to find Tennille and Tate dancing in what appeared to be a world of their own.

"So, I guess it's just you and me," Sterling said and Laila suddenly felt very hot. His voice, unlike his twin brother's, was deep and silky. Laila looked up at him. Although not as tall as Tate, he still towered over her. He had a flawless complexion, a tan from the summer sun, and short, ashen hair pushed messily away from his eyes, making him appear as though he had just rolled out of bed looking this handsome.

"I guess so," Laila smiled at him, unsure of what to think. He appeared so stereotypically preppy when broken down to the basics: blonde hair, athletic build, simple blue button up shirt paired with expensive jeans. But he seemed to have an edge, a glint in his eye that attracted her attention.

Laila struggled to find something interesting to say to Sterling when she felt a tap on her shoulder.

"Hey," a voice said from behind her. She turned around and forced a smile when she saw Julian and his friend Chase.

"You're new here, aren't you?" Julian asked, chewing on a piece of gum while he spoke.

"Yeah. I mean, yes, I am," she said trying to sound as if she belonged at this East Coast preparatory school. They both snickered.

"I'm Julian. This is Chase," he said, taking her hand and kissing it, much like Alistair had done. But unlike Alistair's innocent touch, Laila felt Julian's tongue run between her knuckles, his fingers tightening around hers. She pulled her hand away softly but with enough force to break free.

"I'm Laila. It's nice to meet you." She nodded at each of them, rubbing the back of her hand against her side, suddenly incredibly uncomfortable under Chase's constant stare and Julian's playfully devilish grin.

"Where are you from?" Julian asked.

"San Francisco."

"Surprise, surprise," she heard a voice from beside her say with a whiny, slightly slurred drawl. Kalyn and another girl stepped in beside Julian. "A blonde with blue eyes from California. I'm guessing she's a Democrat as well."

The smile faded from Laila's face. Kalyn looked like she had stepped out of *Vogue*, with teased and highlighted hair, flawlessly applied makeup, and a designer dress. She was model beautiful. Kalyn looked Laila up and down.

"It must be an uncommon thing around these parts, I suppose." Laila said before she could stop herself.

"What, Democrats?" Kalyn laughed and Julian smirked.

"No. Natural blondes."

Sterling, Julian, and Chase laughed. Kalyn simply glared at her.

"Can I get you something to drink?" Julian asked, taking a step toward her and reaching for her waist. Kalyn scoffed and turned away, dragging her friend by the hand toward the exit.

"No, I'm fine, thank you," Laila replied quickly, moving backwards and stepping on Sterling's feet.

"Are you sure?" Julian looked at her through narrowed eyes, glancing at Sterling.

"She said she's fine." Sterling put a hand around Laila's thin arm, taking a few steps back and pulling her with him. "We were just about to sit down before you interrupted us. Why don't you spend some time with Kalyn?"

CHAPTER TWO

Julian shot him a menacing look but Sterling didn't care. He had, on more than one occasion, with and without the help of his brother, put Julian in his place. The look Chase had given the new girl made his blood boil. Chase's eyes had never left her, raking over her body as if she were a piece of meat being presented to a starving mob.

Kalyn scowled and walked away, the crowd parting to let her pass.

Sterling put an arm around Laila's ribs, turning her in the other direction. He glanced behind him and saw Julian motion for Chase to follow him. His friend nodded but he stood as still as a statue, watching Laila walk away, until the people on the dance floor filled in the space between them.

"Thanks for saving me back there," Laila said. Sterling's attention shifted from the two guys behind him to the pretty girl tucked closely to his side. No, not just pretty, gorgeous. And not gorgeous like the other girls at the school who had enough money to hide behind artificially sculpted faces and expensive make up. She was naturally beautiful with long strawberry blonde hair, and small, delicate features. Her nose turned up slightly at the end to give her an innocent appearance, and her perfectly bowed lips were deliciously full and pink. The other girls would rip her apart if she wasn't careful.

"You're welcome," Sterling had to remind himself to answer her. "I imagine you'll want to form your own opinions about the rest of the students here, but those two really aren't the type of guys you want to hang around with."

"I figured as much," Laila said. "They look pretty creepy."

Sterling led her over to a table and pulled out a chair.

"Chivalrous, are we?" He held the chair, waiting for her to sit down.

"It might be considered chivalry on the West Coast, but here we call it being a gentleman."

Laila let out a small, barely audible laugh that sounded like the soft playing of a harp. He sat down, trying to keep his composure. Harp music? What the hell was happening to him? His heart raced as if he had just finished a soccer game and his fingers twitched with a longing to feel the softness of her skin. He looked around the room in an attempt to calm his nerves, noting the whispers and glances from the groups of students still dancing. He saw Randy Showman, the strange ginger scholarship student, staring at the new girl but he quickly stood up and walked away when Sterling caught him. He sighed. Word had probably already spread throughout the class that Laila had stood up to Kalyn. Sterling could only imagine what the girls were whispering about her and Kalyn would surely retaliate. He knew her well enough to guarantee it. Luckily, Laila seemed naïve enough, for now, to be above the swirling shark-infested waters of Harper's.

"You're staring," Sterling commented, as he turned his attention back to her. Not that he minded.

"Sorry. It's just that when your brother said you had the 'crazy eyes,' I didn't understand what he meant."

Sterling let her stare for a moment longer. He used to be self-conscious about his eyes, unsure of how to react when people commented on them. But he had grown accustomed to the attention. It was uncommon but not unheard of for people to be born with two different colored irises. The dark blue of his left eye contrasted with the light green of his right, but in the dimly lit basement, he wasn't surprised it had taken Laila this long to notice.

"They're beautifully peculiar," he heard her say softly as her gaze danced between the two colors. *Beautifully peculiar.* That was a new one and he liked it.

"You're one to talk," he said and she blushed and looked away.

"No, no, no. You saw mine, now let me see yours," he teased as he reached for her face, turning it back to his.

Laila tried to resist, then gave up and opened her eyes wide. He held her chin in his hand and moved closer.

"Kalyn called them blue, but they aren't. Are they violet?"

"I'm impressed you're able to tell the difference in this light."

"Well, now that I've noticed, it's becoming increasingly difficult to look away," Sterling smiled and she blushed again. He could tell she hadn't been complimented much, which was amazing considering her beauty.

"Violet eyes are far less common than what I have." He watched her long lashes blink in what seemed like slow motion. Did this girl have any idea what she was doing to him? He glanced down at her seductively pouty lips, though he didn't think she intended for them to be so, and he couldn't stop himself from running his thumb over their pink fullness. But the second he touched her mouth, she pulled away from him and sat back in her chair.

"I'm sorry," he said quickly. "I didn't mean to–"

"You don't need to apologize," Laila interrupted him. He was relieved to see she didn't look mad. "You just surprised me, that's all."

"So, California?" Sterling quickly changed the subject.

"California," Laila admitted, almost as if she was embarrassed by it.

"What brings you all the way to Harper's?"

"I want to go to Yale. More students from Harper's Prep are admitted to Yale than any other private school on the East Coast. And certainly more than any on the West Coast."

Sterling smiled. Both of his parents were Yale alumni and he had never imagined going anywhere else for college. Alistair, on the other hand, had dreams of a big city and had upset their parents by announcing he was applying to Harvard and NYU. Yale was his backup.

"Did you go to a private school in San Francisco?"

"I did. Not a boarding school, like this one, but it was private."

"Let me guess, an all-girls Catholic school?"

Laila frowned. "Yes."

Sterling laughed. "Don't worry, I won't tell anyone."

"It wasn't that bad," she insisted.

"Well, I think you'll be just fine here. Keep flinging insults at Kalyn Andretti and you'll be famous in no time."

"She's not going to let that one go, is she?"

"Probably not. But I wouldn't worry too much about it. She's harmless unless you're susceptible to catty comments and gossip."

CHAPTER THREE

Laila knew she could handle anything but she wasn't looking forward to dealing with catty chicks and their drama. Her last school had been so small compared to Harper's. There were only 35 other girls in her class, not enough to distinguish between the popular kids and the picked on. But it was clearly different here in Massachusetts, where the money was as old as the prejudices.

Her parents were well off and more concerned about how far from home she was than Harper's steep tuition. But their money was nothing compared to the wealth of the other Harper's parents. She had been shocked at who appeared when she Googled Harper's Alumni after she had been accepted.

"Laila, would you like to dance?" Sterling asked.

She frowned and glanced at the dance floor. The majority of students danced close, arms and legs tangled, hips grinding against hips, breasts pressed to chests. She didn't know how to dance like that and was embarrassed at the thought of even trying.

"I'm not a very good dancer, Sterling. I've never even been to—"

"Wait!" he cut her off, an excited grin on his face. "Don't tell me this is your first dance."

"It's not. I've been to dances before—very chaperoned, very sober dances."

He laughed and she had to smile. His brother had the dimples but Sterling's smile was in a league of its own.

"Come on, then. I'll ease you into it."

Reluctantly, Laila stood up and Sterling took her hand. He led her to the dance floor and chuckled as she looked around uncomfortably.

"Just look at me," he leaned in and whispered into her ear. He put his hands on her hips and pulled her close, wrapping his arms around her back. She leaned into his arms and raised her head to look at him.

He danced well and she felt awkward in his arms. She knew they looked ridiculous but he didn't seem to mind. She tried to relax and enjoy the moment. He pulled her closer and Laila felt goosebumps ripple up her arms. Her breathing felt shallow and a warm blush spread over her face. Sterling handled her boldly but delicately in a way that both calmed and excited her nerves and prevented her from pulling away. She tilted her head back so she could look at Sterling. Faint stubble dotted his chin above his lip, though the hair was so light she could barely see it. He had a straight, rather legal looking nose, set perfectly between his fascinating eyes. She looked away quickly when their eyes met. Taking direction from one of the other girls on the dance floor, she rested her face against Sterling's chest. He smelled nice.

She inhaled deeply and closed her eyes, wishing it was a slow song, or wishing she had paid attention to Gabrielle's instructions. Her sister was on track to become a professional dancer but her many attempts to teach Laila had failed miserably. Laila just didn't have the coordination,

She felt her dance partner push her hair to the side and she felt his warm breath on her shoulder. His hands lightly touched her arm and her lower back, clenching the material of her dress softly in its fingers. His lips on her neck didn't startle her as much as they scared her. Laila felt terrified because instead of wanting to scold him for his bold move, she actually wanted his lips on her skin. She tilted her head to the side, allowing him to continue. She knew this shouldn't be happening but she was too wrapped up in the moment to consider how she should be acting in front of her new classmates, to consider the impression she was making.

Her heart pounded. Sterling hadn't stopped with just a single kiss on her neck. He had pulled her closer still, his mouth moving along her jaw, dangerously close to her lips. Laila had to make a choice. She could allow this boy to kiss her, this boy she hardly knew, this boy whom she would have to see in classes for the rest of the year, who would most likely tell his twin brother and all of their friends about how he had kissed the new, crazy girl from California the first night of school—or she could run away.

She took a deep breath and made her decision. She reached for the back of Sterling's neck and closed her eyes as their lips met. It was as if a thousand pounds of tension had been released and Laila relaxed, if only for a second, believing she had made the right decision.

Bliss.

And then came the realization of what she was doing on her first day at a new school. This wasn't how she behaved. How could she let her guard down so quickly?

"I'm so sorry," she blurted out, their faces still close together as panic overwhelmed her body. "I never act like this. I don't know what came over me."

She spoke quickly and started to back away from his embrace. But he held her tight, not ready to let her leave.

"I don't either," he smiled at her reassuringly. "We were caught up in the moment. No harm done."

"I should go," she said, putting a hand on his chest and pushing him away.

"Laila, you don't need to leave. I don't want you to go," he said in a hushed voice.

Her face reddened and she looked away, checking to see if anyone had seen them. But all the couples on the dance floor seemed to be caught up in their own erotic foreplay, some way more indecent than what she and Sterling had just done. She saw one boy's hand roaming under the shirt of his dance partner. Laila felt her throat tightening and tried to calm her breathing. She would look foolish using her inhaler now. Another couple kissed passionately beside them. The music played slowly, lazily, adding to the charged atmosphere of the party.

"I'm just not the type of girl who does these things. I should go," she repeated, taking a few steps away from him, her mind winning the battle over her body.

He caught her hand before she could get away. "I can tell you aren't that type of girl. And that is what I like about you." Her cheeks reddened more and she knew she had to leave. Now. This was all too much, too fast. "I'll see you later, Sterling."

"At least let me walk you back to your room."

But Laila shook her head and smiled at him. "Goodnight."

She dropped his hand and pushed through the dancing crowd, skipping up the stairs and disappearing from view.

CHAPTER FOUR

Laila walked as fast as she thought she could manage through the dormitory, her heels clicking along the hardwood floors, the sound reverberating through the hallway. She needed to get to the safety of her room before her better sense wore out and she ran back to Sterling.

Chills ran up her spine as she rounded the corner. She thought about the way his hands had felt on her – strong and curious.

Laila closed her door and locked it, walking quickly to stand in front of the mirror above her dresser. She studied her reflection carefully, trying to discover exactly what Sterling had found so appealing. The dress itself was pretty average and certainly not revealing. It came to her knees and had a somewhat modest neckline. She ran her hands over her stomach and felt the material, like Sterling had done. Pretty standard stuff. She shook her head and reached behind her shoulders to unzip her dress, shrugging it from her shoulders and letting it fall to the ground.

Although she didn't want to, she knew she would be feeling his hands on her all night unless she took a shower. So without another glance in the mirror, she wrapped her pink robe around her and stepped out of her panties and heels, exchanging them for a pair of plastic shower sandals. She had been here for two days already, but things still seemed foreign. She didn't like sharing a shower with the rest of the girls on her floor, even though there were more than enough stalls to go around. She felt lucky to have a roommate as great at Tennille, but missed the privacy of her own room as well.

Laila peered out from behind her door, glad to find the darkened hallway empty of students. She walked quickly to the showers, opening the door quietly and slipping inside. She chose the last stall, painfully aware that her silhouette would be visible from behind the textured glass. She was thankful the showers weren't communal. That loss of privacy would have been too much for her to tolerate. She would have had to shower at three in the morning or some other ungodly time and even then she would be uncomfortable.

She closed her eyes and let the warm water run through her hair. Even the water couldn't remove the feel of his touch on her skin. She shivered and froze.

"Did you see Sterling Pierce with Tennille's new roommate?" said a whiny voice.

"Jealous, Kalyn?" A second voice teased.

"Hardly," Kalyn replied, not too convincingly.

"Julian seemed to notice her, too," a third voice chimed in.

"Yes, well, Julian notices anything with boobs and a vagina." The three girls laughed and Laila waited to see if they would say anything else. She could hear the sinks turning on and off, water splashing, and electric toothbrushes humming.

"But seriously, who does she think she is?" Kalyn asked her friends, her mouth sounding full of toothpaste. "I mean, she just shows up our senior year, hell-bent on being a bitch?"

"You were the one who started it," one of the girls said.

"Whatever, Tasha. She's just some ugly, West Coast hippy, with bad hair and an inflated ego."

The three of them laughed and Laila sighed, trying to decide whether or not she should confront them. She didn't have time to make up her mind. The laughter faded and the door closed. Laila turned off the water as soon as she was sure they had left and stepped out of the stall, grabbing her robe and pulling it around her.

She took her time flossing and brushing her teeth, trying not to let Kalyn's words hurt. But looking in the mirror, she couldn't help cursing her reflection. Her light eyes looked dead without make up on her blonde eyelashes. Her skin was so pale it was almost translucent and her body was too thin for her liking. But sports were hard for her with her asthma and she was stuck with Yoga or Pilates to keep healthy.

Laila walked slowly back to her room, passing doors with names of students she didn't recognize scribbled on white boards and collaged from magazines, convincing herself that she was better than Kalyn and her friends. The girl really had no reason to dislike her, though she supposed she hadn't done much to defuse the situation. *Natural blondes.* Laila smiled at her comment though she knew she should be reprimanding herself for it.

She needed to make friends at this school, not push people away. Kalyn had probably attended Harper's since her freshman year and most likely knew everyone. She seemed like the type of girl others would look up to, maybe envy. The entire female population would know exactly how she felt about Laila, come Monday morning.

Laila slipped into her room and closed the door, locking it and resisting an urge to call her mom and beg for a plane ticket home.

She rested her forehead against the back of the door. "You can do this, Laila." *Yale is worth it.*

"You can do what?"

Laila jumped and screamed at the deep voice behind her.

"Darn it, Sterling! You scared me half to death."

"Sorry." He didn't look apologetic at all. He had exchanged his jeans and button up dress shirt for a plain white tee and flannel pajama pants. The short sleeves of his t-shirt highlighted his strong, muscular arms. Arms like that only existed in the movies, or on action heroes in comic books.

"How did you get in here?" Laila asked, trying hard not to imagine Sterling in a tight spandex body suit equipped with a cape and mask.

"You left the door unlocked."

"Well, please leave."

Sterling took a few steps toward her and stared down into her eyes. "Alistair laid claim to the room tonight. I've got nowhere else to go."

Laila stared at him, completely bewildered, because clearly he thought that was a reasonable excuse. "What about Tate's room?"

"Where do you think Tennille is?"

"Is his roommate going to let himself into my room as well?" This guy had an excuse for everything, didn't he? She wished she didn't find him so attractive. His unruly confidence aside, Laila felt her heart beating faster as she remembered the touch of his lips.

Sterling laughed. "Matt, I'm sure, has his own backup room. You'll find that on the weekends, no one really stays with their designated roommates."

"What about the proctors?" Sterling laughed at her question. "Please. They're off doing their own thing. As long as no one dies, we can do pretty much whatever we want. It's called 'building responsibility.'"

"It sounds like negligence."

"Our parents want us educated and admitted to the best school. As long as Harper's does that, it's doing its job." She really had a lot to learn.

"So, did you just assume my room would be the best place to crash for the night?" She was starting to tire of this game, or perhaps just starting to give in to him. He really was quite charming, the way he smiled at her.

"I always stay here. Tennille had her own room for most of last year after the big scandal between her roommate and one of the math teachers. Since Tennille was always in Tate's room, I was able to come and go as I pleased." Sterling took a few more steps in Laila's direction, reaching for the belt of her robe and twirling it through his fingers.

"The math teacher slept with a student?"

"Yup," he said as if it was nothing at all. This place was like some strange, new planet. She didn't know if she could breathe in its atmosphere.

"As you've already noticed, Tennille has a new roommate who most definitely doesn't want strange guys staying with her."

"Most definitely?" His hand rose to her face and brushed some of the damp hair from her eyes, tucking it behind her ear. "I like the way you speak. It's endearing."

"And that's condescending."

"Not condescending, appreciative."

"Look, Sterling," Laila said, turning away from his hand and walking across the room. "It's bad enough what happened in the basement earlier tonight. I just got here. I don't need to give the other girls anything more to gossip about. "

"Did someone say something to you?"

34

"I heard Kalyn and some of her friends talking about us in the bathroom." She bent over, opened her dresser drawer and noticed Sterling trying to take a peak. He was incorrigible.

"Is there an *us* already?" Sterling sat down on her bed.

"Up, up, you're not sitting there." He didn't move, just sat there with a cocky grin on his face. Did she even want to get rid of him? "They were mostly talking about me, I guess," Laila said, turning back around and giving up the fight, a pair of purple shorts and matching cotton top clutched in her hand.

"Did they call you ugly and poor?"

"An ugly, West Coast hippy with bad hair and an inflated ego."

Sterling laughed and shook his head. "Kalyn's just jealous. Everyone who isn't her friend is either ugly or poor. She probably didn't like the attention Julian was giving you, either. "

"That's what I keep telling myself. But I really don't need to make any enemies right now. This year's going to be hard enough as it is." She stood awkwardly beside her bed.

"Just ignore her. She'll eventually leave you alone."

Laila stared into his eyes. She felt relaxed with him, even without make-up and going-out clothes on. The banter soothed her and she liked his confidence.

"I need to change," Laila said.

"Okay," Sterling grinned at her.

Laila waited for him to turn around or close his eyes but he didn't.

"Are you waiting for something?"

"You think?" Laila retorted, her hands on her hips.

Sterling looked proud of himself as he turned around and put a hand over his eyes. Shaking her head at his cockiness, Laila waited before stripping off her robe, wanting to make sure he wasn't going to surprise her and peak through his fingers. But he didn't. Maybe there was some gentleman in him after all. She pulled her shorts and tank top on quickly before throwing back the covers of her bed and sliding underneath them.

"Okay, you can turn around now."

Sterling turned toward her and opened his eyes. He stared at her.

"Your eyes look beautiful right now," Sterling said softly as he started to crawl his way up her bed.

"I never wear purple out in public. It's my favorite color but it makes my eyes look…strange." Why was she telling him these things? Suddenly she wanted him to know everything about her; she wanted to know everything about him.

"Funny, the same thing happens to me when I wear purple." Sterling grinned at her and she laughed, not so much from his joke but more from how crazy the whole situation felt. She wanted him to kiss her again, but she didn't want him to come any closer. He was on her bed. What would he expect from her if she let him kiss her right now?

"You should go to Tennille's bed now. I'm ready to turn the lights out."

Sterling looked shocked. "I can't sleep in her bed."

"Yes, you can," Laila answered, curious to hear his excuse.

"I could, I suppose, but I don't want to. I don't want to for the same reasons I would never sleep in Alistair's bed or Tate's. I know what goes on between the sheets."

"Okay, gross." Scenes from CSI Miami with black lights and obscene amounts of bodily fluids flashed through her mind.

"Exactly. So, you couldn't possibly make me sleep there."

"You'll have to sleep on top of the covers then. You aren't sleeping with me."

But Sterling was already pulling back the sheets on the other side of the bed. "Come on. There is plenty of room. You won't even notice I'm here."

"Nope." Laila pulled the sheets away from his hand and wrapped them around her. "You're lucky I'm letting you stay here at all. I could call campus security and have you removed."

"You really aren't going to let me sleep with you?"

"Not tonight, I'm not." He lifted himself onto his knees, looking down at her as she sat against the headboard.

"Can I ask for a goodnight kiss, then?"

"That's rather bold of you," she said but her pale cheeks blushed pink.

"It is," he agreed with a smile. They stared at each other for a long moment.

"I'm not after anything more, Laila, just a kiss."

She rolled slowly onto her knees and leaned toward him. He smiled as she bit her bottom lip, nervous about what she was about to do. Sterling kept his hands down at his sides until she was merely inches from him.

"Close your eyes," he whispered, taking her face in his hands.

She blinked once before closing them, her lips pulling tight and then relaxing as she waited for his kiss. She felt the kiss first on one corner of her mouth and then the other before their lips met and sealed. The kiss remained gentle from start to finish. Electricity fired through her body. She had studied chain reactions in physics and this was it: uncontrolled, runaway explosions. Their lips met again, and again, and she didn't want it to stop.

"Wow," Laila breathed when they finally parted for air. Her lips tingled.

"My feelings exactly," Sterling grinned as he opened his eyes to look at her.

She took a deep breath. "No one has ever kissed me like that."

"I've never kissed anyone like that before." Sure, like she was supposed to believe that.

"Goodnight, Sterling. For real this time."

"For real?" he teased her before turning off the lights. The glow from the outside lights dimly lit the room.

"Whatever, go to bed." She laughed in the darkness.

"As if," he countered.

He drew back only the top quilt of Tennille's bed.

"You're deplorable," she yawned. He looked adorable, stuffed into Tennille's bed with her rose colored sheets and his long legs stretched out and almost off the end of the bed. This was bad, she realized. She wondered how many other girls he had sweet talked, how many other girls he had seduced with his confident charm. Could she trust him?

She fell asleep replaying the last kiss in her mind, a smile on her face.

CHAPTER FIVE

Sterling woke up to Laila's light breathing. He rolled onto his side and stared at her from across the room. Her head rested gently on her pillow, her strawberry blonde waves flowing across it. Her lips were parted slightly, a faint smile resting on the corners. Sterling didn't want to, but he knew he had to get up. Glancing at the clock on the wall, he knew Alistair and he would be late to meet their parents. But that didn't faze him. Last night was worth it. Waking up to Laila's perfect face, undisturbed and wonderfully peaceful, was excuse enough not to set an alarm clock.

He slid out of the bed, quiet as a whisper, and made his way to Laila's desk. The girl already had her books organized and her notebooks assigned. Purple Post-It notes were meticulously organized, telling her exactly where to go and what to bring her first day of class. He picked up a pen and jotted a note for her, silently removing it from the pad and pressing it to her nightstand before he left the room.

*You look beautiful in the morning. I can't wait to
see you again…*

Sterling passed only a few people on his walk
back to his dormitory that morning. Most were girls
doing their walk of shame, mascara smeared on their
face, shoes in their hands. When he finally made it to
his room, he lifted the tie from the door knob and let
himself in. Alistair was lying on his back, his arms
behind his head, a crooked smile on his face and his
eyes closed. As he heard the door shut, his eyes flew
open and he scrambled to the head of his bed.

"Jesus, man! What the fuck do you think the tie is
for?"

Sterling looked at the bottom of the bed and saw
two manicured feet sliding under the covers and out
of sight.

"Still? It's nine in the morning and you two have
had all night."

Alistair gave him a guilty grin. "Morning wood,"
he said with a casual shrug of his shoulders. "She
offered to take care of it for me."

"Alistair, you're such an asshole!" Rebecca's
familiar voice came from under the navy blue
comforter.

"Good morning, Rebecca," Sterling said.

"Morning, Sterling." Rebecca's brown curls
bounced as she slid up the bed and rested her head on
Alistair's chest, a slightly guilty smile on her pretty
face. Alistair twirled a strand around his finger before
sitting up and kissing her forehead.

"Babe, Sterling and I have to leave. We're expected at our parents' place in less than an hour."

"All right, I get it," Rebecca said, reaching for her shorts which hung from Alistair's bed frame. Sterling knew that, more than anything, Rebecca wanted an invitation to go with them. For years she had been asking to meet their parents but Alistair refused. Alistair didn't want to commit. He knew he could have Rebecca anytime he wanted, spend as much time with her as he pleased, in and out of bed. His brother was always waiting for something better to come along.

Rebecca pulled her shorts on and leaned in to kiss him. "We'll finish this later?" she asked quietly, trying to sound seductive.

Alistair kissed her again and smiled.

"Of course."

Rebecca grinned, hopped off the bed and skipped past Sterling on her way out the door.

Sterling waited until the door had closed before reprimanding his twin brother. "How many times are you going to break her heart before you realize you two belong together?"

"Belong together? Please, you sound like Mom. And she knows what she's getting every time she comes home with me."

Sterling rolled his eyes and went to his closet, picking out a clean shirt and a pair of cargo shorts.

"Where did you stay last night, anyway?" Alistair stood up and stretched before finding some clean underwear from his drawer.

"Tennille's room, as usual."

"Tennille's room? Was her new roommate there? God, that girl is hot."

"Laila. Yeah, she was there." Sterling smiled. Of course she was there. He would have slept in the common room if she wasn't.

"And? How was she? I bet she can fuck like a college girl. All those West Coast girls can."

"You have never slept with anyone who lived west of Ohio, so how would you know?" Sterling demanded, slightly uneasy at his brother's crude way of discussing Laila.

"So I've heard," Alistair answered, winking at his brother.

Sterling rolled his eyes and tossed a clean pair of socks onto Alistair's bed. His brother hadn't done laundry in weeks.

"Thanks." Alistair sat on the bed and pulled the socks on. "But you didn't answer my question. How was she?"

"I wouldn't know," Sterling admisaid. "She made me stay in Tennille's bed."

Alistair threw his head back and laughed. "That's so shitty!"

"I'm pretty sure she's a virgin. A far cry from most of the girls at this place."

"That's the damn truth," Alistair said.

"I don't know. There's definitely something different about her."

"You like her, don't you?"

Sterling turned his back on his brother and reached for his deodorant, waiting until he had applied it before speaking again.

"So what if I do?"

"So, I think that's great."

Sterling turned around and looked at his brother. Alistair had never been one for relationships but everything about his statement seemed sincere.

"Thanks, Al."

"You're welcome. Now, let's go. Mom's going to kill us when we get there so we might as well get it over with."

Sterling nodded in agreement and grabbed his car keys from his desk. Knowing Alistair, he was probably still drunk from the night before.

CHAPTER SIX

"Oh my God! What did the note say?"

Laila blushed and handed it to her roommate.

"'You look beautiful in the morning. I can't wait to see you again!' Shit, girl, you've already got this boy wrapped around your finger!"

"I don't know if it's really like that. He was just trying to be sweet."

"Exactly! Sterling Pierce isn't sweet. Sure he's nice and a gentleman. But no girl would actually describe him as sweet. He usually doesn't give anyone a second glance, even if he's trying to sleep with them."

"Do you think that's all he's doing with me? Trying to get me into bed?"

"I seriously doubt it. If he didn't get into your panties last night, he would have given up already. But this," Tennille waved the purple post-it note wildly in front of Laila. "This is ground breaking!"

Laila laughed. She couldn't help it. Her head was telling her to keep away from Sterling, but her heart and her body said something else entirely. The goofy grin hadn't left her face since she woke up that morning and read his note. She couldn't wait to see him again.

* * *

"Miss Roberts? You can come in now."

Laila stepped confidently into Mr. London's office. She had exchanged emails with him before arriving at Harper's but had never met him face to face. She had imagined him as tall with dignified gray hair and glasses. The image of a prep school guidance counselor. The actual Mr. London was probably thirty pounds overweight and short. He stood behind his desk, his pudgy hand extended for hers, a warm smile on his round face. She liked this version better.

"Hi, Mr. London. It's really nice to finally meet you."

"Likewise, Miss Roberts. Please, sit."

"Thank you." Laila smiled at him and sat down in the plush chair across from his desk. Too plush, she thought. The cushion nearly enveloped her and she squirmed awkwardly in the chair until she was perched on the edge, her feet just barely touching the carpeted floor.

"So, tell me. How was your first week at Harper's Preparatory?"

"It's different than St. Mary's, that's for sure," Laila offered. "But I'm making some friends and the work load seems manageable."

"Well, I would hope so. You've taken half the classes already."

Laila blushed. That was true. She had intended on graduating early from St. Mary's and had overloaded on credits her junior year. But Harper's acceptance letter had made her change her mind.

"Are you homesick? Transfer students, especially those who aren't accustomed to the boarding school life, often find themselves missing the comforts of home more than others."

"I am. The whole roommate thing is taking some getting used to, but Tennille is really great. I could do without the communal bathroom but I suppose it's a good warm-up for college."

"And how are you finding life in the Northeast? Have you had a chance to leave the campus and see the town?"

Laila nodded her head. She and Tennille had escaped the cafeteria one evening and found a pizza parlor just off the small square in the middle of town. "I like how laid back everyone is in town," she told Mr. London.

He grinned. "Can't say the same for the students, can you?"

Laila smiled. "Not really. It just seems like everyone is in a hurry and even though they seem curious about me, very few of them have even attempted to speak to me. If it weren't for Tennille, I don't know if I'd have any friends at all." She decided to leave out any mention of Sterling.

"I felt the same way when I started working here. Most of the other faculty is from the Northeast and if we hadn't shared a similar passion for education then I'm not sure I would have lasted very long."

"Where are you from?" Laila asked politely.

"Not too far from where you grew up. Sacramento."

"Really?"

"Born and raised. I moved out here after I graduated from UC Davis."

"So I'm not going crazy?" Laila asked. "The people here are way different from the people in California? My mom said it was probably all in my head because I was the new girl at school."

"It's probably a little bit of both."

"Hmmm," Laila pondered this a moment and then shrugged. "I guess I'll just have to get used to it."

"I'm sure you will," Mr. London laughed. "Especially if you plan on going to college out here. Yale, isn't it?"

"That's the goal. And that's why I'm here today." Laila was ready to cut through the small talk. Sterling had asked her out to dinner and she was eager to see him again. Ever since that first night when he had stayed in the room with her, he seemed to be all she could think about. She was actually glad when classes started because she had something to take her mind off him.

"What can I help you with, then?"

"Well, you know what Yale is looking for so I was hoping that you could help me find ways to improve my transcript." She glanced at the rows of college brochures which lined Mr. London's shelves. Harvard, Yale, Stanford, Oxford, Brown. Only the best schools in the world for the students of Harper's Prep. She wondered how many of the students actually deserved admission and how many paid their way through the doors of higher education.

"Laila, you're a straight-A student with a near perfect SAT score. There's not a whole lot more you can do other than become captain of a sports team, or student body president."

Laila shook her head. Neither of those ideas was realistic. "Isn't there something less participatory I could try?"

Mr. London laughed. "Yale likes leadership. But they also like community service and the ability to prove your knowledge. Have you thought about tutoring underclassmen?"

"I could do that." She liked the idea.

"Lucky for you, it pays as well," Mr. London said, reaching into his desk and looking through his papers.

Laila smiled. She didn't need extra money but it would be nice to have some cash to spend without her parents being able to see her purchases on her credit card statement.

"What subject interests you?"

"Anything I guess. What has the highest demand?"

"Physics and chemistry."

"Sign me up for physics, I guess."

"Okay, I'll do that."

Laila stood up to leave. "Thank you for all your help."

"It's my pleasure, Miss Roberts." Mr. London stood up and walked her to the door, holding it open for her. "I'll let you know when there's a student in need of a physics tutor. It shouldn't be more than a few weeks, I imagine."

"Thanks again." Laila smiled at him and shook his hand. "Later."

"Good evening."

Laila walked through the door and ran straight into Kalyn, who glared at her.

"Sorry," Laila murmured as she walked around the girl. Kalyn's head tilted in a regal nod.

"Ah, Miss Andretti, what can I do for you today?" Mr. London's voice faded into the background. Laila left the waiting room and turned into the hallway. Despite her run-in with Kalyn, Laila was on cloud nine. Yale was within her grasp. Sterling would be a pleasant distraction. He sat next to her in English and again in History, their only two classes together, and was attentive and studious. More positive qualities.

She walked up the steps to the room and heard Tennille playing the violin. The notes flew through the hallway, rising and falling. Tennille didn't have talent, she had a gift.

Laila opened the door quietly and watched her roommate swaying in time with her bow, her shoulders flexing in exaggerated movements as she played.

Tennille opened her eyes as Laila shut the door.

"That was beautiful!" Laila gushed. "What was it?"

"A Tennille Kelly original."

"Serious? You wrote that?"

"Impressed?" Tennille laughed.

"Incredibly," Laila laughed as well. "Do you have any more that you've written?"

"Only a few dozen, or so. But that one is my favorite."

"What's it called?"

"I call it *My Only.* I wrote it the night Tate told me he loved me. The first time we…well, you know."

"That's so romantic," Laila blushed.

Tennille put the violin back in its case and sat down facing Laila.

"So what about you? Ever been in love?"

"Me? No. Not yet."

"And what about Sterling? Could he be the lucky guy who steals your heart?"

"Maybe," Laila admitted, looking down at her feet with a grin. "Tennille," she asked after a moment's pause. "Can I ask you a question?"

"Of course."

"If it's too personal, just tell me and I won't be offended…"

"Laila, nothing is too personal for me. I'm an open book."

Laila smiled. She liked that about Tennille. There were no secrets, no hidden agendas, just pure honesty.

"How did you know you were ready to sleep with Tate?"

"Oh! That's an easy one. I realized one day, after we had been together for a couple of months, that I trusted him and loved him completely. I was a virgin so I wasn't going to throw myself at him. I made him wait until he was fully committed."

"Did he know you were making him wait?"

Tennille laughed. "We didn't talk about it, but I think he knew. But he's not the type of guy to lie about loving me just to get me into bed."

"Clearly. You two are practically perfect together."

"Practically, but not quite."

"What could possibly be wrong in your relationship?"

"Ha! I could name a thousand things that are wrong in our relationship. We fight all the time because we are so similar, both stubborn and bullish." Tennille shook her head and smiled. "But for everything that is wrong with us, there are a million things that are right. And whenever I'm upset with him, I play his song and remember how much I love him."

"Wow, I really never expected to hear you say something so incredibly sappy." Tennille laughed at her sarcasm.

"Whatever, Miss I'm-keeping-Sterling's-note-in-my-underwear-drawer!"

Laila laughed and stood up. "Speaking of, I have a date."

"So that's what all the questions were about! Are you thinking of sleeping with Sterling?"

"What? No! We're dating. I guess, I don't know. I'm still not sure if he's serious about me."

"Yet he's been here every evening this week and can't keep his eyes off you."

That was true. "We may be headed towards something more, but for right now, I'm holding on to my V card."

Tennille laughed. "You don't know what you're missing. But you hold on to it for as long as you can. It's worth a lot, trust me."

"Thanks, Tennille. Help me pick out an outfit?"

"Of course. Anything for you, girl."

CHAPTER SEVEN

$\mathcal{K}$alyn woke up early, showered, fixed her hair, put on her uniform, applied perfume and make up, and walked to class. Almost a typical day, minus the school bit. This year felt different, though. This year she was a senior and could tell by the looks from the underclassmen, boys and girls alike, that she was going to be queen bee of the school. Not that this surprised her; she had been working toward this title for three years now, eager to accept her crown.

Stepping into English class that morning, she looked around the familiar surroundings. Bench desks lined the stadium style classroom, students already sprawled on the tables in a vegetative state of boredom. But something made Kalyn stop in her tracks. Sitting in the upper corner of the room was Tennille's new roommate, Laila. Aghhh, she was everywhere.

Kalyn hated to admit it, but the girl was cute. She had natural blonde hair with just a hint of red, perfect skin and a hot body. At least Kalyn had bigger boobs.

She glanced down at her cleavage. Her black lace bra was just barely visible beneath a white button-up shirt. Her new, black patent leather heels made her four inches taller. No, nothing was going to ruin her day, especially some prissy bitch from California.

She felt something brush by her shoulder and looked up to see Sterling Pierce walking by.

"Sterling!" Kalyn exclaimed as if she hadn't seen him in years.

"Hey, Kalyn." Sterling's gorgeous eyes looked her up and down. He looked annoyed. She had stared into those eyes many times. The dark blue one had always been her favorite. She missed the way he used to look at her, with love and excitement. That was a long time ago and they had both moved on. At least she pretended she had, but the truth was that Kalyn still harbored feelings for him. How could she not? He was handsome, caring, and more of a gentleman than every other guy in the school combined. With a little persuasion, the fire could be rekindled, she was sure of it. It had burned so hot once. And she needed the excitement and passion before settling into a life of drudgery with Julian. She deserved it, didn't she?

Even though she was only eighteen, she knew that breaking up with Sterling would be one of the big disappointments of her life. And she didn't live with disappointment.

"You look great, as usual," she smiled at him.

"You look like you missed a few buttons on your shirt," was all he said before turning his head and searching for a vacant seat.

"Why don't you sit with me?" Kalyn asked, putting a hand on his arm. "It will be just like old times."

But Sterling shrugged her hand away and glared at her. "Kalyn, it will never be like old times. Now, if you'll excuse me, I've already found a seat."

Kalyn's lips pulled tight and her brow furrowed as she watched him walk up the stairs, straight toward Laila. The new girl raised her head as she saw him, a prissy smile on her face. Ever the gentleman, Sterling pointed to the chair next to her and asked to sit down. Kalyn glared as the blonde blushed and nodded, encouraging him to take the seat. Sterling sat next to her and put his bag on the table, leaning in to her as he did so. He brushed Laila's hair from her face and planted a gentle kiss on her cheek.

"Fucking prissy bitch," Kalyn muttered under her breath as she turned on her heels and walked to the other side of the classroom. Tasha had saved her a seat and Kalyn dropped her books on the floor, slamming herself into the chair and swearing under her breath.

"What's with you today?"

Kalyn looked at Tasha. Her hair was a mousy brown, straight and with the texture of hay. She had constantly pink cheeks and a nose that was too small for her face. Lucky for her, her family had more money than the Queen of England. The girls had grown up summering together and skiing in Vermont. Tasha was the closest thing Kalyn had to a best friend.

"It's that new girl, Laila. She's already getting on my nerves."

"Still her? Get over it, Kalyn. You've only got a year with her." On most days she appreciated Tasha's direct and frank observations. But not today. Today Kalyn felt spiteful.

"I know. Julian just really pissed me off last night and I haven't gotten my period."

"You need me to take you to the clinic?" Tasha asked without batting an eye or bothering to lower her voice.

"No. I'm just PMS-ing."

Tasha rolled her eyes. "What did Julian do, anyway?"

"I caught him in bed with some sophomore. He didn't even bother pulling out. He kept going and casually asked me to come back later."

"Look, Kalyn, I'm only going to say this once this year because you heard it enough last year. You two aren't engaged yet. He's clearly enjoying his freedom and you should be enjoying yours. Why do you even care what he does?"

"Tasha, I'm supposed to marry the guy," Kalyn reminded her friend. "He should want me and only me."

"Why don't you focus your attention on something or someone you actually want?"

Kalyn sighed. The circle kept coming back to Sterling. He was what she wanted. Fuck Julian and their so-called betrothal. She had no obligations to him until they graduated and she wasn't going to let him rule the last year of her single life.

Her eyes focused across the room as the teacher called the class to attention. Sterling watched Laila open her book and push it between them so they could share. Kalyn stared at him until he felt her eyes on his face. He glanced up and their eyes met. Kalyn smiled as innocently as she could manage. Sterling frowned and shook his head before returning his attention to the text book.

She would get him to love her again. He couldn't deny how amazing they had been together, couldn't take back the words he said when he promised to love her forever, couldn't pretend he didn't want her anymore. He was a guy, after all, and half of their brains resided below their beltlines.

CHAPTER EIGHT

"Kalyn, sit up straight. Are they teaching you nothing at this school?"

"It's a high school, Mom. They teach us history and math, not table etiquette."

"We didn't raise our daughter to slouch at the table and talk back to her parents," her father replied. Kalyn slowly straightened her back and flashed a small, pleasant smile. The four adults at the table looked pleased with her change in behavior. She glanced at Julian but he didn't provide any sympathy. He pretended to listen to their fathers' boring discussion, nodding his head at appropriate times.

Kalyn sighed and looked over at her mother. She had hated the woman for years but recently felt only pity. Mrs. Andretti was miserable, though she never let anyone see it. Between dinner parties, spa appointments and her husband's credit card, she hardly had time to think about her life. She drank every evening — at least three tumblers of gin — and constantly tried to please a husband who showed little appreciation. Kalyn wanted to respect her parents but found it an increasingly difficult task. Her mother lived a lie and her father lived off a company his grandfather had built. He probably worked only ninety minutes each day. Kalyn would have felt sorry for them both, but mostly resented them for forcing her into their lifestyle.

The Polks and the Andrettis hadn't ever used the words "arranged marriage" but that was essentially her predicament. At eleven, her parents had told her that she would marry Julian. At the time, Kalyn had thought it just talk, her mother envisioning a Disney-like wedding that united two families. But over time it became clear that marrying Julian Polk was an expectation, pretty much the only expectation apart from perfect manners. It was not just friendship that bound the families but business. To her father, marrying his daughter to his chief business ally's son ensured the future of his company and his income. God forbid he should ever have to actually work for a living. In a sense, she had become his prostitute and piggy bank.

They didn't care if she went to college. Why would a housewife need a college degree? They didn't care if she did well in school. Why does a housewife need good grades if she isn't going to college? On the eve of her sixteenth birthday, a night she planned to spend with Sterling, her mother had told her it was time to "grow up." She needed to end the relationship with Sterling. In a monotone voice, her Stepford mother had explained the consequences if she didn't comply. Of course, Kalyn had thought it was a joke. Her mother wouldn't force to her marry someone against her will. Mrs. Andretti told her that if she wanted to forgo her inheritance, she could marry anyone she wished. At first it seemed like an easy decision for Kalyn. Who needed money? She could make her own. Then she looked in her closet at her designer clothes, thought about the cars and the houses and the vacations she would have to do without. She knew she wasn't strong enough. She liked the high life. And after weeks of thinking about it, she finally called Julian.

"I've known for a while," he had said, surprising her.

"Why didn't you tell me?"

"Because I knew you would freak out. I did."

"What do you want to do?" Kalyn had asked hesitantly. Julian was a good friend; they had practically grown up together and even though she only felt a brotherly-like affection towards him, she didn't want to be rejected.

"It's not like we hate each other," Julian had laughed. "We get along great and, really, what are the odds of either of us being truly happy with the person we marry? Most marriages end in divorce anyway."

"So, you're okay with this?"

"People like us can't be poor, Kalyn. We don't know how to be poor. And like I said, it's not as if we hate each other."

"What am I going to do about Sterling?" She had asked, more to herself than Julian.

"You'll have to break up with him," he said simply. "It would be better to do it sooner rather than later before you are really attached to him."

But she already was attached. She loved Sterling, and even though she was still young, she could picture them together years and years into the future.

"What am I going to say to him? I can't just break his heart."

"Would you really choose Sterling Pierce over your inheritance?" Julian and Sterling weren't particularly close and had gotten into some major rifts on the soccer field, but the two didn't hate each other. Not at the time.

"I don't know yet," Kalyn had answered quite honestly.

"Well, just remember that if you do choose him, you aren't just fucking yourself over, you're fucking me over as well." And with that, Julian hung up. He had been right. It was his life as well as hers and, really, how hurt would Sterling be? They were young and could learn to love again.

Kalyn chewed her food slowly as the dinner dragged on and on, remembering how difficult it had been to make her decision. Her mother asked Mrs. Polk which colleges Julian had applied to, bringing her back to the conversation.

"His first choice seems to be Harvard," Mrs. Polk said, as if Julian wasn't sitting directly beside her. "But he's applied to Columbia and Georgetown as well."

"Kalyn will of course go wherever he chooses," Mrs. Andretti said with a smile and Kalyn wondered when her life would finally be her own. It might never happen. Her throat tightened and tears welled in her eyes. Don't cry now, she told herself. Mother will not like that. She had become a parrot trapped in a cage, forced to look pretty and repeat after others.

Kalyn swallowed the lump in her throat and looked away, catching a short but sympathetic glance from Julian. Those were few and far between nowadays, so the novelty of it gave her a little rush of pleasure. She spent the rest of the dinner in silence, looking at her plate and feeling forgotten. At nine o'clock they were both excused to return to school. Their parents followed them into the foyer and watched Julian help his fiancée with her jacket. He offered his arm and they walked together out to the car. Maybe life with him wouldn't be so terrible. He could be a gentleman when he wanted to be and at one time he treated her with respect and affection. They had been close friends.

"Thank you," she said sweetly as he opened the car door for her.

* * *

"I was thinking about the conversation tonight," Kalyn said as Julian started the car. "About us going to college together. It seems only right that an engaged couple would be attending the same school."

Julian hit the gas and the Porsche screeched out of his parent's driveway.

"You're grades aren't good enough to get into Harvard," he replied coolly.

"So then what's wrong with Columbia?"

"Columbia? Are you fucking joking, Kalyn? Everything is wrong with Columbia."

"If you are determined to go to Harvard, I can always go to Boston University. We can live in the city together."

"Or not."

Kalyn was silent for a moment. "You're right. It wouldn't look good if we lived together before we are married. I guess we should keep up appearances."

"You know, I was thinking," she said, leaning into him and whispering in his ear. "Maybe you could come back to my room and help me blow off some steam. These dinners with our parents always get me so wound up."

"Sorry, I've got plans tonight." Julian kept his eyes on the road.

"With who? That little sophomore slut?" Kalyn pushed herself away from him and slumped back into her seat. She hated that she had been unable to make herself stop wanting Julian. There was just something about him, something that made her want to please him but he always pushed her away. They were both resentful about the situation, that was obvious and to be expected, but at least she was trying. He only made an effort around their parents.

"Does it matter?"

"I guess not," Kalyn agreed. She didn't want to know who or what he was going to sleep with next. She hated most of the girls in her class because they had, to some degree or another, all taken Julian's attention away from her.

Kalyn pulled her phone out of her purse and started texting. *Rough night. You available?*

"Who are you texting?" Julian asked, glancing at her lap where her phone was glowing.

"Does it matter?"

"Look, I can't ask you to stay celibate until we are married and I wouldn't want to. But I don't want a whore for a wife, either. Just make sure the boys you choose to fuck can be discreet."

"You are such a hypocrite, Julian!" He seemed to get a rise out of irritating her, which only made her madder.

"So what if I am? But you better get used to it, sweetheart, unless you want us both to lose our inheritance."

Kalyn crossed her arms and looked out her window the rest of the ride back to Harper's. The trees grew thick as they approached, their leaves starting to change to oranges and reds.

I'm free. Where are you?

Kalyn's phone vibrated on her lap and she shielded the screen from Julian.

20 minutes. Your room.

Kalyn's thoughts wandered as the trees flew by. Breaking up with Sterling had been the hardest thing she had ever done. For Sterling, it came out of nowhere. She couldn't tell him the truth, that she had chosen her inheritance over him, so she let him believe that Julian had stolen her heart. Of course, once the rumors started, Sterling figured it out on his own. He never forgave her.

But Julian had been great those first few months. He let her cry on his shoulder, let her spend the night when she was lonely, and before long Kalyn actually started developing true feelings for him. She was overjoyed the first time he called her his girlfriend, but couldn't help feeling that if things had been different, had their parents not interfered, she would still be happy with Sterling.

Just as Kalyn had started becoming comfortable with their situation, Julian started pushing her away. They would fight and break up; get drunk and sleep together; wake up and be back to where they were the day before. It was a vicious cycle, but at least he was still acting like a boyfriend part of the time. But something had changed in the last couple of months. Julian had become more distant, more resentful. He wanted nothing to do with her.

Kalyn tried to push all this from her mind as she watched Julian walk to his dorm. She waited a few minutes before following, wanting to make sure he didn't see her when she knocked on the door. Chase Nichols was one of the lucky students who didn't have a roommate. He could thank his parents' hefty donations for that, and so could Kalyn.

"Hey, I was starting to give up on you," Chase said as he opened the door. His shirt was already off.

There were no pretenses here. "Did Julian actually learn how to drive the speed limit?"

"Can we not talk about Julian right now?" Kalyn snapped, kicking off her shoes and pulling off her sweater.

"I won't say another word," Chase smiled at her, locking his door and unbuttoning his pants. Kalyn stared at him as he undressed. Chase was thin and lanky, his muscles lean. There wasn't an ounce of fat on him. The chestnut hair on his head matched the small patch on his chest. His face was nothing to write home about. He was average looking, at best, and standing next to Julian, he was practically invisible. Some say he had a nice smile when he actually chose to show it. But Kalyn didn't care about his looks. He could have been completely deformed for all she cared. No, all that mattered was that Chase was Julian's best friend and even though she prayed Julian would never find out about her affair, she knew that her choice would hurt him. Sleeping with Sterling Pierce would have wounded her fiancé the worst, but her ex-boyfriend hadn't been responsive to her advances—yet.

She finished undressing and tried to push all thoughts of Sterling from her mind. She was in Chase's room and would soon be in Chase's bed. She glanced at him and saw that he was already throwing the extra pillows onto the floor. Her lips curled into a smile as he caught her staring and he motioned for her to join him.

* * *

"Do you think someone heard us?" Kalyn asked after the deed was done. She always tried to conceal her moans and screams, knowing that the walls of Harper's Prep were thin and there could be any number of students walking by Chase's room, including Julian.

"Probably," Chase replied, his eyes closed as he lay on the bed.

Kalyn frowned. She didn't know why she even bothered asking because she knew his answer would be an honest one and not the one she wanted to hear. She closed her eyes only for a minute, never being one to linger.

"I'm going to go," she announced, sitting up and glancing at her clothes lying on the floor. She considered telling Chase to go retrieve them for her but knew he would only laugh.

"Feel better?" Chase asked, rolling on his side and staring at her as she climbed out of his bed.

Kalyn smiled and looked over her shoulder at him. "So much better. Thank you."

Kalyn picked up her underwear from off the floor.

"So, how's your senior year so far?" She asked him.

"It's been fine," Chase answered vaguely.

"Yeah? I haven't seen you around too much. Did you find some girl to occupy your time?" Kalyn smiled at him as she pulled her panties up.

"Maybe." Chase watched her clip her bra on. Even he had his weak spots.

"Who is she?"

"Laila Roberts."

Kalyn rolled her eyes and scoffed. "What is it with guys and that girl? Is she really that pretty?"

"It's not just her looks, Kalyn. She's different from the other girls at school."

"Because she's from California? Because she's a virgin?"

"You don't know that."

"Word is that Sterling won't commit to her because she refuses to sleep with him."

"And you would like nothing better than if he started sleeping with you again,"

"Whatever," Kalyn rolled her eyes for a second time. "Look, I saw her name on the board outside of the academics office. She's available to tutor you in physics, if you're interested."

"Physics? I hate physics."

"Well, then, you'll probably need a tutor. Just remember, little miss innocent isn't going to just jump into bed with you. You're going to have to get to know her and be nice to her and all those unpleasant things," Kalyn smiled at him before opening the door and leaving the room.

She heard him muttering to himself as she closed the door: "Maybe a physics tutor wouldn't be that bad."

CHAPTER NINE

The email from Mr. London told her to meet the student in the library at 7:30. She was going to be early, but that gave her time to set up and prepare. Laila wanted to make sure she was comfortable with the material before she attempted to tutor anybody on the subject. She flipped through the pages.

Mass. Force. The Laws of Thermodynamics. If only life fit together as precisely as a physics equation, at least as far as Sterling was concerned. They had been seeing each other for nearly a month now, going out, having steamy make-out sessions in random places all over campus, but she still had no idea about the nature of their relationship. Were they dating? Friends with benefits? God, she hoped that's not what he thought. She wanted to have the conversation but could never quite get the courage to ask him about it. For now she felt optimistic. Life felt good. She didn't want to ruin it.

Finding a seat in the tutoring room, she glanced around. It was large and quiet. There were a few other students and teachers but no one she recognized. She pulled out her physics book, calculator and some scratch paper, trying to look as organized as possible before the student arrived. The door opened and she looked up. Randy Showman walked in. They hadn't spoken much since exchanging hellos the first week of school. Even though his bright red hair made him stand out, people tended to overlook him. Probably intentionally. Money and pedigree determined the pecking order at Harper's, and he had neither.

Laila waved and Randy casually waved his hand back. He nearly tripped over a chair on his way over to her.

"You aren't here for a history tutor, are you?" he whispered when he reached her table.

"No. I'm tutoring physics."

"You doing this for your college application?" he asked. "My advisor said it would help."

"Mine too," Laila admitted.

"What school are you trying for?" Randy sat down.

"Yale. You?"

"U Penn."

"Nice."

"I'd do anything to graduate early, but it doesn't look too hopeful. Harper's isn't too keen on the idea."

"It's not that bad here, is it?"

Randy shrugged. "I guess by now I've grown used to it, but college will be a refreshing new start."

"I don't know how you've put up with the social politics of this place for so long." Even though she spent the vast majority of her time with Sterling, Laila found she hadn't been immune to the gossip that ran rampant through the halls and classrooms. She often caught people staring and whispering when she walked by. Kalyn glared. And more than once she had been asked about her relationship with Sterling from people she barely knew.

"I've been Switzerland. Cold and neutral. Without the money, of course."

Laila laughed and nodded her head. "Well, it's almost over."

"You seem to be fitting in just fine," Randy commented.

"I try to keep out of everyone's way as much as possible. It's easy to do when you're friends with Tennille." Tennille had helped out a great deal, encouraging Laila to thicken her skin and give the gossipers a true piece of her mind. In other words, to tell them to mind their own fucking business. Laila had chosen not to use those exact words but it was nice to know that someone as respected as Tennille had her back.

"And the Pierce twins," Randy added.

"That helps, I suppose." Laila blushed.

"Tennille's great. She and Tate have been really nice to me these past three years. You're lucky to have them as friends."

Laila nodded. "I agree. I can't imagine what life would be like if I were roommates with someone like Kalyn Andretti."

Randy laughed. "I heard she isn't your biggest fan."

"Dude, the girl hates me! The glares she gives me from across the classroom could cut glass. It can't be because of what I said the day of that dance?"

"That probably started it but I imagine her real peeve is that you are with…"

"Um, Randy?" Rebecca Valencourt stood at the end of their table. She looked perpetually unhappy but Laila guessed being friends with Kalyn could do that. Rebecca had an exotic look with wild, curly brown hair, olive skin, and a splash of dark freckles over her nose and cheek bones.

"Rebecca," Randy stammered and stood up. His face flushed and he gave a goofy grin.

"Sorry to interrupt," Rebecca said, looking between Randy and Laila. "But I'm looking for my history tutor. That wouldn't be one of you, would it?"

"That would be me," Randy said.

"Oh. Great." Rebecca smiled at him and then looked back at Laila.

"Have fun," Laila told them as Randy stumbled to pick up his bag and waved goodbye. She watched him pull out a chair for Rebecca and then debate whether he wanted to sit next to or across from her. "Oh great," she sighed when she saw the next person walk through the doors. Chase Nichols. The very sight of him made her skin crawl. In class, he just stared at her

73

all the time like a deranged stalker. She didn't even know what his voice sounded like.

"Laila?" He asked quietly.

"Hi, Chase."

"You must be my physics tutor?" he said.

Laila nodded. She bit her lower lip.

"Great. I hope you're good at this stuff. I'm completely lost."

"Chase, I don't think…" Laila started to tell him she couldn't go through with tutoring him but then stopped. She envisioned receiving the acceptance letter from Yale. She glanced at Chase from across the table. His voice had been so much softer than she had imagined. He looked like he wanted to learn physics. Perhaps she had been wrong about him.

"…I don't think you have anything to worry about." What was it her mother always used to say? Don't judge a book by its cover? Maybe she just had to get to know him a little. He couldn't be that bad, could he?

"Good," Chase said, leaning across the table. "Because I have a secret to tell you."

"What's that?" Laila leaned in.

"I'm failing," he whispered, flashing big doe eyes. "I don't think they'll let me into a good school if I fail." He looked truly concerned but she thought he was just being flip.

"Don't worry. I won't let you fail," she promised him.

CHAPTER TEN

Sterling looked across the large room at Laila. She sat next to a young boy and pointed at the page and then spoke a few sentences. She looked at the boy, her eyes sparkling. Suddenly, she raised her hand, congratulating the boy with a high-five.

Harper's had introduced a new component to the curriculum for senior year: mandatory community service. Each quarter on a rotating schedule, the social studies classes assembled to spend the day doing various good deeds. Today they were at a homeless shelter, and while Laila had the good fortune of helping kids with their homework, Sterling had been assigned to the buffet line.

"Hey, Sterling," he heard an unwanted voice say from beside him. "Or should I say Alistair?"

"Hi, Kalyn," he said begrudgingly as he pulled on his hair net. She clung to him like a tic on a dog.

"What are you doing here?"

He finally looked down at her. Kalyn's hair was pulled into a tight ponytail. He cringed even though she looked beautiful. He had to admit Kalyn looked good doing anything. At one time, he really had loved her.

"Alistair doesn't like doing community service and I don't like taking Econ midterms. This works out better for both of us."

"Well don't worry," Kalyn said with a smile, lightly touching his arm. "I won't tell anyone."

Sterling only nodded his head in feigned appreciation.

"I haven't seen you two pull this stunt since freshman year."

"Mr. Kline is new and doesn't know any better," Sterling said with a smile. The truth was, he and Alistair had been looking forward to switching places since they first learned of Mr. Kline's arrival at Harper's Prep. The other teachers had gotten wise to their tricks long ago.

Sterling glanced back at Laila and wondered if she had noticed yet. She had arrived with the later bus and had smiled and waved at him from across the room. As if she could sense his eyes on her, she raised her head and turned toward him.

Sterling blew a small kiss and winked, causing her to turn bright red and furrow her brows fiercely. He grinned at her bewilderment and could practically see the switch flip in her head as she realized who she was looking at.

Laughing at herself, Laila shook her head and turned back to her student. Sterling chuckled and then looked down at the food he was supposed to be tending.

"What's up with you and Miss California, anyway?" he heard Kalyn ask.

"It's really none of your business," he informed her coolly.

"Oh, come on. Everyone is talking about it and wondering if you two are a couple or merely fuck buddies."

"Laila isn't the type of girl who could earn that label," he replied, knowing very well that Kalyn had earned it with multiple guys.

"Maybe she's just frigid," Kalyn said nearly under her breath.

"Why are you even talking to me?"

She nearly took a step back, seemingly surprised at his outburst. "There's no one else to talk to here," she said as sweetly as she could.

"You're fiancé is just down there," he pointed out, nodding his head toward the end of the buffet line. Julian stood awkwardly and silently next to a very grim looking Randy.

"Well, I'd rather be talking to you." Kalyn batted her eyes and Sterling tried to remember if she had ever done that when they were together. He couldn't remember a time when he had seen it, but then again, he had been too young and naïve to notice if she had been playing games with him.

"Maybe you should pay a bit more attention to your food," he suggested.

"Gross! No! I don't see who could eat this stuff," Kalyn said, louder than Sterling would have liked. A few heads turned their way but she was oblivious to it all and continued to embarrass both of them. "I mean, if I had known I would have been cast into indentured servitude, I would have just had my parents write a check and gotten out of it."

Sterling sighed and looked back at Laila. She laughed at something the young boy said or did. While his ex-girlfriend had once been fun and animated, she was now cruel and manipulative, even when she was trying to impress him. Laila, on the other hand, was kind to everyone and never seemed to have ulterior motives.

The first person walked up to the line with his tray. The man wore an old army jacket and tattered jeans. His hair, or what was left of it, was long and unkempt, and he walked with an obvious limp. Dog tags hung from around his neck.

The man smiled at Kalyn and Sterling as he approached, holding out his tray in anticipation. Sterling smiled back and loaded him up with macaroni and cheese.

"Thanks." The man turned to Kalyn, who frowned before scooping up some beans and practically throwing them on the plate.

"I can't believe we have to be here. Have any of these people even heard of personal hygiene?" she said when the man was only a few feet away.

"Fuck, Kalyn. Just stop talking," Sterling groaned.

She looked hurt, but only for a second. "You know what? I don't need to do this," she announced, dropping her serving spoon dramatically and storming off toward the bathroom as if she expected Sterling to follow her. He watched her leave and then looked around, hoping no one else had seen her tantrum. Randy gave him a peculiar look and Sterling shrugged his shoulders, receiving a small grin from the strange redhead.

He took the silence as an opportunity to return his attention to Laila but she was no longer at the study table.

CHAPTER ELEVEN

"Okay, you work on this problem and I'll check it when I get back," Laila instructed Henry, the adorable 10 year old she had been tutoring for the last hour. The way he stared at her with wide eyes made her feel needed and appreciated.

Henry nodded his head and Laila stood up from the table. She walked to the bathroom and pushed the door open, stopping dead in her tracks as her eyes fell upon Kalyn. The girl who had been so cruel to her that first weekend of school stood by the sink, picking through small white pills which she held in her hand. She picked up three of them and tossed them back, not noticing Laila until she had already swallowed them.

"Well, look who it is," Kalyn said with a fake smile. "Little Miss California."

"Hi, Kalyn," Laila said, the words heavy and uncomfortable in her mouth.

"You know, I think we really got off to a bad start."

As obvious as her statement was, it surprised Laila to hear her say it.

"I was just upset that my fiancé was talking to you but I should have just realized he was welcoming the new student, much like I should have done."

Laila remained silent as she tried to figure out Kalyn's game.

"How are you adjusting to Harper's?"

"I'm adjusting just fine," Laila replied. "Thank you."

Kalyn turned away from her so she could check her reflection in the mirror and Laila took the opportunity to glance at the prescription bottle which still lay open on the sink. She couldn't read the small print but wondered what kind of medication Kalyn could be taking that would allow her to pop three pills at one time.

"Sterling is no doubt helping you through the gauntlet?"

"He's been great."

"Can I give you some advice?" Kalyn asked, her voice hushed. "As someone who has known him for a while?"

"Okay."

"Don't let him play you like this." Laila frowned and Kalyn continued. "I mean, the rumors going around are bad enough to ruin a girl's reputation but you don't want your heart broken as well, do you?"

"What rumors?"

"Oh, sweetie. Has no one told you? They are saying that he is only using you for sex."

"That's not true at all," Laila interjected.

"Well, of course it's not." Kalyn looked as though she was trying to be sympathetic. "But he hasn't asked you to be his girlfriend yet, has he?"

"No," Laila shook her head, suddenly feeling a small twinge of doubt. She had wondered for some time why Sterling hadn't brought up the topic of commitment. Granted, she had never had a real boyfriend before and didn't know how to initiate that kind of conversation or if people even talked about it. Maybe it was just one of those unspoken understandings? Sterling had been giving her all the signs of a boy who wanted to commit to a relationship. They had been spending nearly all of their free time together and he had taken her out multiple times, never allowing her to pay for anything.

"Why are you telling me this?" Laila asked, suddenly curious at Kalyn's concern.

"I don't want to see you get hurt," Kalyn said, her eyes growing glossy.

"Well, thanks I guess."

"Anytime," she answered with a shrug of her shoulders. Kalyn collected her pill bottle from the sink and tossed it into her purse. "And no one needs to know about this conversation. Especially Sterling."

She walked out without another word. Laila couldn't believe that Kalyn of all people could have her second-guessing her relationship with Sterling.

She knew the gossip mill at Harper's ran twenty-four hours a day, seven days a week, but she didn't like the idea of people thinking she was being used for sex. It would take nearly all of her resolve, but she would confront Sterling about where they stood. If he wasn't willing to commit, she wasn't willing to pretend they were more than friends.

Laila pushed open the bathroom door. She would find Sterling on the bus ride back to Harper's and ask him where he saw their relationship going. It would be that simple.

Henry looked up as he saw her approaching, a wide smile on his face. He presented his completed homework.

"You did this all while I was gone?" Laila asked, beaming at her new young friend.

"Will you check it?" he asked.

"I'd be happy to," she answered, completely forgetting her disheartening conversation with Kalyn.

CHAPTER TWELVE

$\mathcal{R}$andy found it curious and slightly discouraging that he felt more at ease in a homeless shelter than he did within the walls of Harper's. While his family never had the means to send him to private school, buy him his own car, or take exotic vacations, they weren't poverty stricken. Growing up, he had known a few kids at the public schools he attended who had spent time in homeless shelters and he had never looked at them with pity. The families were doing what they had to do to survive and were able to land on their feet if they took advantage of all the resources available to people in their situation.

At the shelter, he couldn't help but notice the sense of community. People helping people. That's how it should be everywhere. But the boy standing next to him was a sharp contrast to Randy's ideal world. Julian had fought, nearly tooth and nail, when he had been assigned to the food line. However, after being given a second option of joining the group in the laundry room, he had quickly closed his mouth and picked up his hairnet. Since then, Julian had remained silent, occasionally glancing a few tables down at Kalyn and Sterling (who was doing a horrible job of pretending to be Alistair). Given what he knew about their relationship, Randy was amused to see Julian getting angry every time he watched his fiancée flirt with Sterling.

The kids at Harper's were a bunch of spoiled babies and he hated them for it. He hated the games they played and the massive sense of entitlement. Not even Tennille understood the depth of his anger. Being at the shelter just crystallized his feelings.

"This is such bullshit," Julian muttered under his breath as the first people walked through the line.

Randy knew he wasn't speaking to him and chose not to respond.

"You would think that they would make community service a voluntary part of the curriculum," Julian continued and Randy looked at him, now wondering if his classmate was still talking to himself.

"No one from Harper's would volunteer if that were the case," Randy pointed out.

"That's my point," Julian said roughly. "If we all resent being here, it's just a waste of time. Nothing is accomplished."

"Except for the service and help we are providing."

Julian huffed and both boys watched Kalyn storm off to the bathroom. Sterling looked somewhat relieved to see her go.

"They should learn to help themselves," Julian said.

"That's why they are here," Randy replied trying to keep his cool. How could this guy be such a wad? "They are keeping their children safe and off the streets and they are trying to better their lives."

"Spend a lot of time in homeless shelters, Randy?" Julian asked.

"Fuck off," Randy hissed.

"It's nothing to be ashamed of," Julian insisted with an evil smile. "I bet it's a great place to meet girls."

Randy shook his head, his face turning nearly as red as his hair.

"Granted, there is probably not a lot of privacy but it's better than trying to bone some girl in the bathroom of a McDonalds or wherever it is you can afford to hang out."

Julian elbowed his ribs, trying to provoke him.

"Don't touch me," Randy said in a deadly even tone.

"What would your parents say if they found out? But seriously, if you knocked up a girl at a McDonalds, would you name the kid Ronald?"

Randy clenched his fists and he wished Tennille were here to calm him down. He looked around frantically, trying to find something to distract him from the pathetic excuse of a person next to him. He hated the fact that Julian could infuriate him so easily and normally he would just walk away. But now he was torn between abandoning his class and community service or staying put and listening to the asshole beside him belittle his entire life.

"Speaking of your parents," Julian continued as a large woman with a rat's nest of curly red hair approached. "Isn't that your mom?"

Anger seethed through Randy's head, drowning out all other thoughts. He tried to push it down, bottle it up, but couldn't. The pompous prick's face grinned stupidly.

Randy clenched his hand into a fist and connected with Julian's face. Potato salad flew in every direction as Julian stumbled back, trying desperately not to fall. Randy lowered his shoulders and tackled Julian to the ground, punching his ribs and face as many times as he could manage before Julian started fighting back.

* * *

Julian had expected Randy to retaliate but he had been taken completely off guard by the fist to the face. Randy threw him onto the ground and punched his ribs. The feisty ginger could certainly hold his own.

Julian brought his arms up and pushed on Randy's face with enough strength to force the kid's head back. A swift punch to the stomach sent Randy rolling onto his side and the dynamics shifted. Julian landed one blow to Randy's face before he felt someone pulling him to his feet and dragging him away.

"Get off me, man!" he said to Sterling as he elbowed him in the stomach. Sterling let out a gasp before throwing him to the ground and standing between the two combatants. Randy struggled to stand up but both knew that the fight was over. They glared at each other, waiting for someone to do or say something.

Out of nowhere, Julian saw Laila Roberts sweep in and fall to her knees in front of him.

"Your nose!" she said with her soft voice, a grave look of concern on her pretty face. Realizing that his mouth was full of blood and his head was starting to spin, Julian gladly accepted her help. She shed her cardigan and dabbed it against his nose, searching his face for a reaction.

She touched his nose lightly with the soft material and Julian cried out in pain. She pulled away quickly and he saw that the sleeve was already covered in blood.

"You should apply pressure," she said gently and handed him the sweater. He nodded his head in thanks and held the pink cashmere to his nose.

Laila turned her attention to Randy, who sat on the ground fuming. She gently examined his rapidly swelling eye. Randy winced and turned his head away.

Looking around, Julian could see a crowd had gathered and he wished his head would stop spinning. If he had a concussion, he would be sent to the hospital and Randy could kiss Harper's goodbye. They would expel him. As much as Julian didn't like the scholarship kid, he hadn't wanted to ruin his future by provoking him into a fight. The kid had a temper.

He remained on the ground, leaning against the table leg for support, until Sterling offered his hand to help him up.

"Are you all right?"

The hair at the back of Julian's head stood on end.

"I'm fine, Kalyn."

"I can't believe he would just attack you like that. What a sociopath."

"The kid is crazy," Julian agreed with her, though he felt guilty about the whole incident.

"You should press charges and get him expelled. No one wants him here, anyway."

Julian looked over and saw Randy shrug his shoulders at something Laila said. She reached for his arm, touching him gently, and Randy looked appreciative. Kalyn was wrong. Randy, the person who had started the physical fight was being comforted by his friend. And who was by Julian's side? Kalyn, his fiancée, whom he detested more and more with each passing day.

"It's not worth the trouble," Julian said scathingly, pulling Laila's sweater away from his face and finding a clean spot, free of blood.

"That looks really bad," Kalyn said as she reached for his face. But Julian pushed her hand away and returned the cardigan to his nose.

"Don't pretend you care," he hissed at her and walked off toward the bathroom before Mr. Kline could make his way through the crowd.

CHAPTER THIRTEEN

aila walked up the steep stairs of the charter bus. The driver tipped his hat and she waved. It was, in her opinion, a little excessive to have a bus equipped with leather seats, TVs, a bathroom, and a tuxedo clad driver, to drop them off and pick them up from a homeless shelter. A simple yellow school bus would have sufficed anywhere else but at Harper's.

She looked down the aisle and saw Sterling wave a hand at her. Still shocked at how long it took her to notice the brothers had switched places that day, she walked quickly to claim the seat next to him.

"Exciting day, wasn't it?" he asked her, lifting her hand and kissing her knuckles. He was always such a gentleman in public though she believed he used the gesture simply as a way to touch her. When they were alone, his hands never left her and they had been caught in compromising positions multiple times by both Alistair and Tennille.

Laila blushed as she thought about the last time they had been alone. Sterling had pulled her into his room after class and they hadn't even made it to the bed before his hands found his way under her shirt. Her body tingled at the memory of that afternoon but she needed to stay strong. She had gotten carried away and now rumors flew through the student body. She was determined to put a stop to them.

"Alistair is going to be sad he missed it," she said, pulling her hand away.

Sterling looked dismayed but continued chatting. "How was your tutoring session last night?"

"Fine," she said curtly, wishing she had the courage to initiate the conversation and not act so catty.

"Tell me again why you are doing it?"

"It looks good on my application to Yale."

"You know, my dad plays golf with the dean of admissions," Sterling said, catching Laila rather off guard.

"What?"

He nodded his head. "They were fraternity brothers. I could have my dad speak to him, if you like." Sterling looked pleased with himself.

"No thanks," she said confidently.

"It would get you out of tutoring," he pointed out.

"Sterling, I can get into Yale on my own," Laila told him.

"I know you can," he said, giving her a serious stare. "I just don't like leaving anything up to chance."

"Leaving things up to chance?" Laila repeated in a bitter tone. "Things like me getting into a good school? Thanks for your concern but I can get myself into college."

"I meant things like us being together next year."

"Oh," she said in a whisper, dropping her head to hide her blushing cheeks.

This was the opening she had been hoping for but now she was too embarrassed to speak.

"I didn't know you felt that way," she said eventually and raised her head to look at him. His blue and green eyes stared at her with a mixture of hopefulness and confusion.

"Of course I feel that way," Sterling told her as if she should have known. "What way did you think I felt?"

Laila gave him an apologetic look. "I don't know. We've never talked about it."

"That's kind of an awkward conversation to have," he said, frowning at the idea of it.

"Apparently it is," Laila said with an uncomfortable laugh.

"Well, then, "to avoid future confusion and to make this as clear as possible, I am 100% committed to you, Laila. You are the only one I want and the only one I will be with. It would kill me to see you with someone else."

Laila blushed a deep crimson, nodded her head and looked down at her lap. "That's very good to hear."

"Hey," he whispered, lifting her chin so he could kiss her lips, "promise me the same?"

"Oh, I promise," Laila said quickly and they both smiled.

"I feel like the luckiest guy at school," he told her and put his hand just above her knee to give her a loving squeeze.

Laila reached up and kissed him again, longer and more sensual this time.

"Get a room, you two," someone said behind them. Laila quickly pulled away and blushed again, burying her face into his chest.

CHAPTER FOURTEEN

"Kalyn, this is the third time you've come to see me for the exact same thing." Nurse Emily reprimanded her again. The first time, the nurse had been sympathetic. The second time, she had been concerned. But this time, she was angry.

"I know. And I'm really embarrassed that I have to come back here. But, honestly, I was safe this time. The condom broke."

"The condom broke?" Emily stared at her skeptically.

"Yes," Kalyn lied, trying to look ashamed. In reality, she wasn't ashamed. Just annoyed.

"Kalyn, you have to understand that the morning after pill isn't the safest or the most effective form of birth control. You should be on the pill."

"I don't want to gain weight."

Emily laughed. "You're 18. Most girls your age don't experience any weight gain, and, in the slight chance you do put some on, it will be minimal. Five pounds at most."

Kalyn knew she wasn't going to get Nurse Emily off her back unless she appeared remorseful. She looked at the ceiling and then down at her shoes. "I'm just...I feel so lost. I didn't even want to sleep with him this time but I knew that if I didn't, he wouldn't like me anymore."

"Oh, sweetie," Emily appeared to be falling for her fake tears and her made-up cry for help. "If he really thinks that way then he isn't worth your time."

Kalyn put her hands to her face to hide her smile. What a predictable answer.

"I know," she said between forced sobs. The idea of having Chase Nichol's offspring growing inside of her was enough to make her start crying, but the sex had definitely been worth it. Kalyn went to the school nurse out of convenience and knew that she could drive into town to the free clinic and obtain the exact same prescription. If Nurse Emily wasn't going to help her, it wasn't like she was completely out of options.

"Okay, I want you to promise me something," Emily requested.

"What is it?" Kalyn didn't look up.

"I'll write you this prescription, but I'm also writing you one for birth control. Promise me that you'll consider it."

"I will, thank you." Kalyn glanced at her through watery eyes.

Nurse Emily pulled the prescription pad out of her drawer, scribbling on two pieces of paper and tearing them off, handing them to Kalyn.

"Do you need a few minutes? You're welcome to wait in here for a while."

This was exactly what Kalyn had been waiting for. The plan fell into place. Nurse Emily was so predictable. She nodded and then buried her head back in her hands.

"All right, stay as long as you need."

"Thank you," Kalyn whispered. "I really am sorry."

"There's nothing to be sorry for. Just take care of yourself."

Kalyn nodded and waited until she heard the door close. Her blonde head flew up and she looked at the pieces of paper in her hand. Nurse Emily's writing was elegant and unique but easily forged. Kalyn jumped off the exam table and opened the drawer, pulling out the stack of prescription papers. She tore one off and placed it above one of hers, pulling a pen from the jar and tracing the information onto the blank sheet verbatim, everything but the patient's name.

Completely proud of her work, Kalyn skipped out of the infirmary and back to the dorms. She walked into the bathroom and left the slip of paper near the sinks. She slid into one of the stalls, waiting for a group of girls to come in.

It only took a few minutes before Kalyn heard the door open and voices flood the bathroom. Perfect. An entire group. She quickly flushed the toilet and walked out of the stall, assessing the crowd. Jenna, a girl who had followed Kalyn around all junior year like a pathetic puppy dog, chatted with two other girls she didn't know. Kalyn walked to the sinks, exchanging smiles with the girls.

"Hey, Jenna. How are you?" Kalyn asked as she washed her hands.

"I'm good, thanks." Jenna's smile widened and Kalyn knew that she felt honored to have the queen bee speaking to her. "How are you?"

"I'm great," Kalyn answered with a smile. "I love those shoes by the way."

"Thanks. I picked them up last week when I was visiting my sister in New York."

Kalyn smirked. "You've got great taste."

Jenna, clearly flattered, ignored her friends who were coming out of the stalls.

"Well, it was good chatting with you," Kalyn said, tiring of the conversation, "I'll see you around."

Jenna beamed at her and nodded her head. Kalyn walked toward the door.

"Wait, Kalyn. You forgot something," Jenna said. She turned around slowly to see the girl pick up the prescription from the sink.

"Oh, that's not mine," Kalyn said with a patented, innocent look.

Jenna shrugged and Kalyn watched her flip over the paper to read the other side. Jenna's eyes opened wide and Kalyn walked confidently out of the room.

That should do it. By the end of the day, everyone would be talking and the bitch would be packing her bags and heading back to California. Which would leave Sterling to her.

CHAPTER FIFTEEN

$\mathcal{R}$ebecca sat alone in the lunch room, slowly picking at what was left of her salad, and moping. Her thoughts turned to Alistair, of course. She was furious that he hadn't called in such a long time, but proud of herself for not giving in and showing up at his door in the middle of the night.

Students milled about the busy cafeteria, the long tables filled with seniors trying to pack in as much studying as possible before completing their college applications.

It would be nice to be away from this place, Rebecca thought. Away from the temptation of Alistair Pierce and away from the catty gossip of Kalyn Andretti. She had let herself get sucked into that world long ago, back when she was new to the school. Kalyn was instantly popular, no questions asked, and it was just fate that made them lab partners that first year in biology. They became fast friends, and Kalyn, Tasha and Rebecca were soon nearly inseparable. The three of them would spend hours gossiping about boys, shopping, watching movies, doing what normal teenage girls did.

But all of that changed once Kalyn started dating Julian. It shocked everyone because she had been so happy with Sterling.

Rebecca knew Julian's reputation, but they had been friends and he had never attempted to hit on her. Because of this, Rebecca had been able to see a part of Julian that many didn't, his humanity. But when he started dating Kalyn, something changed in both of them. They became resentful and cold. Kalyn spent hours and hours in front of the mirror, styling her hair and fussing with her makeup, something she never bothered with before. Julian started sleeping around more than ever, not even bothering to hide it from his girlfriend.

And that's when the rumors of an arranged marriage had started. Rebecca didn't believe it at first, but Tasha knew their families and eventually confirmed the rumors as true. It was like something out of the Middle Ages. In a way, she felt bad for Kalyn but it had become increasingly difficult to sympathize with her. Kalyn became cruel and vengeful toward any girl who Julian or Sterling paid any attention to. They remained friends, just barely.

"Hi. Rebecca?"

Rebecca looked up to see Laila Roberts smiling at her from across the table.

"Hi." Rebecca looked at the new girl with an uncertain smile. Kalyn certainly had her mind made up about her, but the rest of the class seemed less certain: her parents had money, she was strikingly beautiful, and she had won the heart of Sterling Pierce.

"May I sit with you?"

"Um, sure," Rebecca stammered, slightly surprised at the request.

"Thanks," Laila sat down and set her tray on the table. "This cafeteria is so big; it's easy to feel completely alone in here."

"I know what you mean."

"So, where are you from?" Laila took a bite of her apple and Rebecca glanced at her tray — apple, a few carrot sticks, and a handful of pumpkin seeds. A carton of soy milk hadn't been opened yet. California diet all the way.

"Connecticut," Rebecca answered.

"I've heard it's beautiful there."

"It is. Have you never been?"

"No. Not yet," Laila said.

"You should check it out sometime. There's more to do in New York or Boston, of course, but Connecticut has a certain charm to it."

"I can't wait, then."

"What part of California are you from?" Rebecca asked with curiosity.

"San Francisco."

"Do you see a lot of celebrities?"

Laila laughed. "Most of the celebrities are in L.A. But I did see Robin Williams at Whole Foods once."

"That's it?"

"You know, I'm not really that perceptive. Most of the time I wouldn't recognize a celebrity if I walked by one. I don't think I would have even seen Robin Williams if I hadn't nearly rammed him with my shopping cart."

Rebecca smiled. She could see why Sterling liked Laila so much. She didn't take herself too seriously and had a self-deprecating sense of humor—a rarity at Harper's where everyone was caught up in their own importance, or lack of it.

"Are you going to invite Sterling out there some day?"

Laila blushed and Rebecca regretted saying it. "Sorry, I didn't mean…"

"No, don't be sorry," Laila interrupted. "It's just, we are taking it slow and I don't know if he's ever going to go to California with me. Should I ask him?"

"Well, why not? You like him, don't you?"

Laila laughed again. "I really, really like him. I've never felt this way before and, don't tell anyone, but it's almost a little bit scary."

"Well, I think it's adorable. You two make a great couple."

"How long have you known Sterling and Alistair?" Laila asked, picking up two pumpkin seeds and popping them into her mouth.

"I guess since freshman year," Rebecca sighed, remembering the first time she laid eyes on Alistair Pierce in orientation. She saw his dimples across the gymnasium. He had grown up so much since then.

His hair was shorter, and his body had filled out – nicely. He had put on a lot of muscle since then.

"Is that when you and Alistair first started dating?"

Laila's question surprised her. Is that what she thought they were doing? "Alistair doesn't date," she clarified but offered no further explanation. "I don't know why I'm so stuck on him. But I just always seem to forgive him whenever he breaks my heart, which is practically every week."

Laila gave her a sympathetic smile. "I guess you can't help who you fall in love with."

Damn. Laila had admitted she wasn't very perceptive, so her infatuation with Alistair must be more apparent than she had thought. But she liked Laila. She liked her honesty and she liked her innocence. Did everyone in California open up so quickly? Laila was naïve about the Harper's way – keep your eyes on your enemies and your secrets close. She knew that their conversation would stay confidential. Kalyn would have already blabbed it across the school.

"No, you can't. Sometimes I wish that I didn't love him as much as I do. Things would be so much easier. But, honestly, there's just no one else who even comes close."

"No one?" Laila smiled as if she didn't believe her. "You can't think of one person at this school who could distract you from Alistair?"

Rebecca thought about it. She didn't really talk to many guys besides Alistair and occasionally his brother. Randy had been tutoring her for nearly two months now and she looked forward to their Thursday evening sessions. She admired Randy's brilliance and appreciated that he didn't make her feel inferior. She had also grown to find him attractive. He had beautiful green eyes and a sincere, infectious smile. But Randy Showman came from a different world and if she dated him, the rumor mill would be in high gear. Admitting she found him attractive could ruin her reputation, whatever that was worth. Kalyn would never speak to her again and Alistair would just laugh.

"Believe me, I've looked. I guess I'll have to wait until college."

Laila grinned and changed the subject. "College. I still can't believe that it's less than a year away now."

"I know!" Rebecca laughed. "I feel so grown up!"

"Right? I mean, *it's college*."

"Rumor has it you are going with Sterling to Yale," Rebecca teased her.

"I had made up my mind long before I met him that I was going to Yale. It's really just a coincidence."

"A really convenient coincidence."

"Exactly," Laila laughed.

"Speak of the devil," Rebecca smiled as the Pierce twins walked up to the table. Genetic miracles. Handsome faces and tall, muscular bodies made them quite a sight to behold.

"Were you talking about us?" Sterling sat down and kissed Laila on the cheek.

"Just girl stuff," Laila smiled at Sterling and Rebecca felt a pang of jealousy. She had, so many times before, looked at Alistair that same way. But he rarely reciprocated the feeling. She would catch him, on very rare occasions, looking at her as if she actually meant something to him. But those instances were few and very far between and always in the privacy of a bedroom. In public, Alistair hardly showed any affection. She was his bedroom girl.

"Where have you been lately? I haven't seen you." Alistair sat next to Rebecca at the table and popped a chip into his mouth.

"I've been busy with college applications and stuff," she replied. She had been avoiding him. He was like a drug to her and she found that after awhile, if she didn't sleep with him, the withdrawal symptoms lessened. It had been nearly three weeks since she had kissed him, nearly a month since they had slept together, and the pain was lessening each day.

"You have plans for the weekend?" Alistair asked, holding a sandwich in his hand but not eating.

"Not really," she said shortly. They both looked across the table and watched as Sterling reprimanded Laila for not eating enough.

"Rebecca, I've missed you."

Rebecca sat up straight. Had she heard him correctly? Her brown eyes turned toward him in shock.

105

"Can I see you this weekend? Maybe take you out somewhere?" He looked nervous. Was that possible?

Before she could say yes, his attention turned to Sterling and Laila.

"This Sunday? Are you sure?" Laila blushed.

"Of course I'm sure," Sterling laughed. "They've been dying to meet you."

"I'm going to be a nervous wreck," Laila whispered and Sterling leaned closer to her. Rebecca's stomach tightened into a knot.

"My parents will love you, don't worry."

"Okay, I guess I'll go. Of course."

Sterling kissed her.

Rebecca turned away before their kiss ended. Alistair chomped on his sandwich, an uncomfortable look on his face.

"So," Rebecca said, raising her voice so the entire table could hear. "Where did you want to take me?"

"Um, the movies?" Alistair asked, his mouth full of food.

"Right." Rebecca flipped her curly hair over her shoulder as she stood up. "I don't think so."

She picked up her bag and shot Alistair a hateful glare before turning to Laila. "It was really nice talking to you, Laila. I'll see you in class."

"All right." Laila looked at her and then at Alistair, sensing the tension. "I'll see you later, then."

* * *

Rebecca walked into an empty stall and threw her bag on the floor, rummaging through it until she found the razor she kept hidden in the side pocket. She removed the blade and pulled up her skirt, tearing off some toilet paper. She pulled the razor slowly across the tender skin of her inner thigh causing a trickle of blood to emerge on both sides of the blade. She winced and when the pain became unbearable, she couldn't stifle a gasp. Blood ran slowly down her leg and dripped into the toilet, swirling the water to pink. Slowly, her body relaxed, her anxiety faded. She knew that no matter what was going on in her life the blood would always be the same–lazy and meandering, soothing and comforting. The pain pushed away all of the other negative emotions and left her free.

She started wiping the blood away and saw Kalyn's patent leather heels outside the stall.

"Rebecca?" Kalyn tapped lightly on the door. "Are you okay?"

"I'm fine, Kalyn. Go away."

"Is it Alistair?"

Rebecca took a deep breath. Of course it was Alistair. Wasn't it always? Sterling barely knew Laila and he had already invited her to meet his parents. She had been with Alistair for years and he invited her to–the movies.

"No," she lied.

Kalyn had Julian. Well, she would have Julian. And now she could have any boy she wanted. Kalyn didn't understand rejection. She would only rub it in Rebecca's face.

"What's wrong? Come on, you used to be able to tell me anything." Kalyn fluttered to other people's misery like a moth to flame. Rebecca realized now that seeing other people down made Kalyn feel better about her own situation.

Rebecca threw the razor back into her purse and closed her eyes, a few tears slipping from between her lids. "It's nothing you would understand," she said, before exiting the stall and walking briskly out of the bathroom. Things needed to change.

CHAPTER SIXTEEN

"Hey, Randy!" Tennille smiled as she sat down.

"Hi," Randy whispered.

"Guess what?"

"What?" He looked up from his homework and gave Tennille an annoyed glance.

Her face beamed with happiness. "I got in to Juilliard!"

Tennille waved the letter in front of Randy's face and bounced in her chair. He grabbed the letter, knowing how much it meant to her. She had auditioned last month, barely making it to New York in the cold November weather, and performed her heart out. Tate had called it the performance of a lifetime but Tennille had been modest, and worried about getting accepted. Randy never had any doubts she would get in.

"Congratulations!" he said, reading the acceptance letter and then carefully folding it back into the envelope. "Have you told Tate?"

"Of course! But I had to tell you second. So, come on. Let's get out of here and go celebrate!"

"I can't, Tennille. Not right now." He wanted to go, but...

"And why not?"

"I'm preparing," he looked back at his books.

"Preparing for what?"

"My tutoring session."

"With Rebecca?"

"Yes."

"You like her, don't you?" Tennille finally lowered her voice to a whisper and moved her chair in.

"Maybe," Randy admitted.

"You should ask her out."

"Tennille, leave me alone."

Tennille just rolled her eyes. "Randy, talk to me about this. You know I can help."

"How? How can you help me?" Randy knew that Tennille found dating to be rather simple. Then again, if he had her good looks, he might find it simple as well.

"I don't know. I can give you advice or something," Tennille said with a curious frown.

"Advice? Okay, I'm listening."

Tennille perked up. "Well, how often do you see her?"

"Every Thursday at 7:30."

"That's it? You need to see her somewhere social," she whispered.

"How can I do that without asking her out?" Randy almost dreaded the answer.

"Come with me and Laila to the party tonight."

"No," Randy's voice was firm.

"Why not? You know she's going to be there and you know I won't stop bugging you until you agree."

He thought for a moment.

"Just tell me that you won't do anything to embarrass me," he finally conceded.

"I promise!" Tennille stood up and smiled.

"Tennille, seriously. Don't embarrass me."

"I swear." Tennille said, bending down and kissing his red hair. "See you in my room in two hours. Don't be late!"

* * *

"Laila! We have to talk!" Tennille threw open the door and rushed inside the room to find Sterling and Laila on the bed.

"Sorry, sorry, sorry!" Tennille said, making her way through the room to her desk while trying to cover her eyes. Sterling groaned in annoyance and Laila giggled with embarrassment.

"What's up?" Laila asked, sitting up and pulling her t-shirt down.

"You will never guess what Randy just told me!" Tennille exclaimed, setting her bag down and spinning to face her roommate.

"What?" Laila's face was still flushed. She pushed Sterling's hand from her waist.

"He just admitted to me that he has a crush on Rebecca Valencourt."

Laila giggled again but Sterling looked shocked. Tennille knew, along with everyone else at school, that Alistair and Rebecca had been messing around since freshman year. Alistair had taken her virginity and her heart but had never committed to the relationship. He probably felt possessive about Rebecca, but at the moment, Tennille didn't care. Randy and Rebecca needed each other.

"Sucks for Randy," Sterling said.

"And why is that?" Tennille demanded.

"Rebecca would never go for someone like him. If you haven't noticed, she's still in love with my brother."

"But she's looking for someone else. She is open to the possibility," Laila said.

"How do you know that?" Sterling asked.

"She told me."

"He's agreed to go with us to the party tonight so we have to help him." Tennille said.

"I thought the four of us were going together," Sterling protested.

"We'll see you two there." Tennille dismissed him with a flip of her hair as she sat down at her desk.

* * *

Laila walked to Rebecca's door, knocked quietly and waited.

"Laila, hi," Rebecca answered, looking surprised.

112

"Hey, I was wondering if you wanted to walk to the library with me."

"For tutoring?" She looked hesitant for a second and then nodded her head. "Okay, why not." Laila waited outside while Rebecca gathered her things.

"Thanks for asking," Rebecca said as she closed and locked her door. "It's getting so dark out now. I kind of hate walking by myself."

"I know what you mean. I always feel safe on campus but there's just something about the old buildings that give me the creeps."

The two girls walked down the hallway and out into the bitter cold.

"So, how is Randy as a tutor?" Laila asked as soon as they had stepped outside. The wind cut into their exposed cheeks and lips.

"He's a great tutor!" Rebecca answered. "He actually makes history fun."

"Do you know where he's going to school next year?"

"Um, he said something about U. Penn. I think he's applied for early admission. He's really smart, you know? And not just book smart. It's like, he just gets it. Gets everything."

Rebecca seemed to know quite a bit about him already.

"I feel so bad for him sometimes," Rebecca admitted.

"Why?" The girls shuddered as a strong gust of wind blew through their jackets and jeans.

"Well, besides you and Tennille, the guy really doesn't have any friends. I just don't understand it."

Laila frowned. How did Rebecca not know? People like Kalyn and Julian singled him out and kept him down for not having as much money as the rest of the class.

"Maybe all he needs is a little encouragement. He's really shy, you know."

"He is shy. But he doesn't need to be. I mean, he's smart and funny, at least some of the time, and he could be attractive if he learned how to dress."

"We could help him," Laila suggested, eager to see Rebecca's reaction. "We could dress him up, teach him how to flirt, maybe even find him a girlfriend by the end of the year."

"Do you really think he would allow us to do that?" Rebecca frowned.

"I think he would if you were there," Laila said coyly.

"And what does that mean?" Rebecca asked, picking up the pace.

"Nothing," Laila insisted once they were inside the library. "I just see the way he looks at you while you two are studying. He seems to think very highly of you."

"Really?"

"Honestly."

"Look, he's coming with me and Tennille to the party tonight. Why don't you say hello. See what happens."

"Why not?" They walked in and saw Chase and Randy sitting at separate tables.

"Just don't tell him our plan or he may not go with us," Laila told her before they parted ways.

"I'll see you tonight." Rebecca walked over to Randy. He flashed a silly grin.

CHAPTER SEVENTEEN

ℜebecca leaned over the sink and applied the liquid eyeliner. She preferred doing her makeup in the privacy of her own room. There were too many underclassmen running in and out of the bathroom at any given time, but the lights were much brighter. She closed her eyes to let the liner dry and cringed when she heard Kalyn's drawling voice.

"Rebecca? What are you doing in here?" Kalyn laughed and Rebecca heard heels clicking across the floor.

"Doing my make-up, Kalyn. You?"

"Waiting for Tasha. She ate too much and needs to throw up before she starts drinking." Rebecca opened her eyes and looked at Kalyn. They hadn't spoken in weeks and she didn't particularly feel like starting now.

"Happy birthday, by the way," Kalyn said. Rebecca put down her eyeliner.

"I didn't think you remembered." In years past, Kalyn and Tasha had decorated her door, sent her balloons in class, made her feel like it truly was a special day. But this year there had been nothing.

"Of course I remembered," Kalyn smiled sweetly at her. "I mean, you only turn eighteen once. What kind of friend would I be if I didn't remember?"

"You didn't say anything all day," Rebecca reminded her. "I just assumed you forgot."

"I've been so busy, you know? Coordinating college applications with Julian."

"Of course," Rebecca said with a weak smile. Tasha walked in and started tweaking her hair in the mirror.

"Hi Tasha," Rebecca called.

"Are you going to the party with Julian tonight?"

"I'm sure he'll be there," Kalyn said quickly. "Are you going?"

"Yes."

"But you're getting ready by yourself? I assumed you would be getting ready with Laila or I would have asked you to join me and Tasha."

"I'm meeting her there," Rebecca said, turning back to the mirror to apply her mascara.

"You know, it's really nice of you to befriend her the way you did. The poor girl really needed some help."

"She's not a charity case, Kalyn. She's actually a really nice person."

"Whatever. It's your reputation. You did hear about her by the way?" Kalyn asked.

"Hear what?"

"Jenna told me she found a prescription in Laila's name for Plan B," Tasha said rather loudly, considering the subject matter.

"Plan B?"

"You know, the abortion pill."

"That's not possible," Rebecca said, shocked.

"Someone might want to tell Sterling that our little miss innocent might not be so innocent." Kalyn turned around and checked her backside. "So don't expect me and Tasha to sit with you two at lunch or at graduation. Some of us still have some pride and dignity and a girl like that just shouldn't be allowed at Harper's."

Rebecca glared at Kalyn through the reflection of the mirror. Her mind still reeled from what Kalyn had said. Laila had told her she was taking it slow with Sterling.

"Did you see the prescription?" she asked. Kalyn smirked.

"I didn't see it, but Tasha did." Tasha nodded and Rebecca knew that while Kalyn might lie, Tasha wouldn't.

"Don't look at me that way, Rebecca." Kalyn turned to face her. "I'm just being honest. She's a lying viper."

Honest? "Okay, then can I be honest with you as well?"

Kalyn looked amused. "Why not? I would love to hear what Rebecca Valencourt has to say about me."

"I don't want you to sit with me at lunch or at graduation. And I don't care about my reputation. Everybody knows me as Kalyn's friend, her sidekick even. And these days, that isn't such a good thing. I'm done with that. Why do you think that the only friends you have left are me and Tasha? Why do you think Julian sleeps with every girl in this school except for you?"

Kalyn scowled.

"How very hateful, Rebecca. After everything I have done for you, this is what you say? After I tried to protect you from Laila. Yes, well, when Julian and I are married and vacationing in the south of France, you will still be chasing after Alistair Pierce."

Rebecca smiled and collected her make-up from the counter. Kalyn's comeback had been all that she needed to end the conversation, and their friendship.

"That is a possibility," Rebecca agreed. "But I seriously doubt it."

CHAPTER EIGHTEEN

*M*usic drifted lazily across the basement. It was still early in the night and the party's vibe felt mellow. It would pick up later. Randy, Tennille and Laila walked down the stairs and into the dark room. Strobe lights danced slowly across the walls, sending shimmering patterns across the seniors.

Randy glanced hesitantly around the room. People never hassled him when he came with Tennille but he still felt like an outsider. Tennille and Laila had done their absolute best to dress him up and style his hair, to turn him into "a guy any girl would want to screw" as Tennille had so crudely put it. Laila had assured him that he looked very handsome.

The three of them started across the dance floor to the punch bowl when Randy spotted her. Rebecca walked towards them, brown curls bouncing over her shoulders and framing her beautiful face. She looked breathtaking in a gold dress with a dangerously low neckline. The hem reached just above her knees. A wide sash accentuated her slender waist and highlighted her shapely legs.

"Hey, Rebecca." Laila greeted her with a hug. She gave Laila an awkward hug back. Strange body language, Randy observed. Something was going on. Randy didn't know when it had happened but Rebecca seemed to have dumped Kalyn and grabbed Laila as her new best friend. It was a serious upgrade in his opinion.

"Hey," Rebecca said with a sad smile on her face. "Laila, I need to talk to you."

"Can it wait?" Laila whispered, nodding her head toward Randy.

Randy noticed people staring at them and felt seriously uncomfortable. Maybe this had been a bad idea. Why was everyone staring?

"Of course," Rebecca said, seeming to force a smile. She turned to Randy. "You look really nice tonight."

"Thank you," Randy said, clearing his throat and praying his voice wouldn't crack from the attention. "You look beautiful, as always."

He could have sworn her cheeks turned red. Randy couldn't remember the last time he had made a girl blush. Rebecca looked like she still wanted to say something to Laila but Tennille cut her off.

"Okay, so let's get some punch and join this party, shall we?" Tennille said. She grabbed Laila's hand and pulled her away from Randy and Rebecca. He noticed some girls pointing at Laila and

121

snickering. The other students weren't staring at him, their eyes and conversation were focused on Laila. What was it about this school? He put the negative thoughts out of his mind. Tonight, he would be calm, cool, confident, and positive.

"After you," Randy said, gesturing for Rebecca to follow the girls. He tried to remember everything Tennille had told him, the subtle ways he could touch her, the right words to say, but his mind had gone blank.

He noticed the small of her back and the curve of her hips and let instinct take over. Randy lightly touched her side, guiding her to the drinks. She didn't push his hand away which had to be a good sign.

Tennille and Laila had drinks in their hands by the time Randy and Rebecca made it to the table. Randy didn't particularly like alcohol but Tennille had advised him to have a drink to lighten up a bit. He didn't want to look like a prude. Rebecca eagerly took the cup he offered her.

"So," Randy said, taking a sip and swallowing the bitter liquid before he could gag. "Do you have any plans for winter break?"

"I'm going back to Connecticut for Christmas and then to Miami for New Year's," Rebecca said.

"Miami?"

Rebecca laughed. "My parents love that place. I don't get it."

"At least you'll be somewhere warm."

"Exactly! I can work on my tan."

Randy studied Rebecca's face. Dark lashes framed big, almond shaped eyes. He noticed a hint of sadness.

"It's great to see you out tonight, Randy." Rebecca said, shyly.

"Thanks. I'm glad I came." He took another gulp of his drink. And he was. Rebecca was actually paying some attention to him.

"Do you want to dance?" she asked.

"I'd love to." he said. She took his hand, dragging him to the dance floor.

Tennille had given Randy a quick lesson on how to dance with a girl after she had dressed him that evening. He had practiced on Laila because she was closer to Rebecca's height, but all Randy had managed to do was turn Laila bright red and throw her into multiple laughing fits. Thankfully, dancing with Rebecca was different. She moved gracefully and held him close, almost dancing around him instead of with him. He touched the soft skin of her arms and pulled her closer as his hand wrapped around her waist. Rebecca swayed her hips with the music.

She threw him a shy smile that looked incredibly sexy. He fought the urge to kiss her. Not yet, he told himself. If he moved in now, he would be like every other pig at the school. Take your time. Rebecca's arms stayed around him as a slow melody drifted through the speakers. He relaxed his step to stay in time with the music and enjoyed the feeling of

Rebecca's hair against his neck. She rested her face on his shoulder.

"It's my birthday today," she said softly.

She looked a bit dejectedly into the crowd.

"Happy birthday," he told her, hoping that was what she wanted to hear.

She sighed and tightened her arms around his neck. "You know what sucks about it?"

"What?"

"I'm eighteen years old today and the people I care about most don't even know it. And the people who know aren't worth caring about."

Randy frowned. Tennille was the only person at Harper's who knew his birthday, apart from Mr. London, but a guidance counselor didn't count.

"I'm sorry, I shouldn't be telling you this," she said, lifting her head from his chest and staring at him.

"I don't mind."

Rebecca frowned. "No, I don't know you that well and I don't want you to think that all I do is complain about how pathetic my life is."

"Can I tell you something?" Randy asked as he took one of her hands so that he could lead her in a more formal dance. Tennille had done her job well. Rebecca stumbled at first but smiled as she finally found her footing.

"Of course." He spun her slowly and brought her back close to him. Other couples stared at them. Perhaps they didn't expect Randy to know how to dance. Maybe they just hadn't expected to see him there at all, much less in Rebecca Valencourt's arms.

"Ever since I started tutoring you, I've had you up on this pedestal. Before I met you this year, you were one of those girls who were untouchable, perfect in every way possible. Then I actually spoke to you and you were so kind and so humble that it only confirmed my vision of you. Hearing that you have insecurities, hearing that your life isn't entirely perfect, well it makes you more human to me. It makes me like you even more."

Her brown eyes widened at his compliment. She didn't say anything.

"I don't want to freak you out or drive you away," Randy continued, "but I've been meaning to tell you, actually, I've been dying to tell you just how beautiful and brilliant you are. You're truly an amazing person and I'm lucky to have met you."

Tears welled up in her eyes.

Great. Now he had blown it.

Her hips stopped swaying and her hands moved from his waist up to his neck. She stood on her toes and pulled his head down to hers, their lips just barely touching. Rebecca gave him a soft, tender kiss.

Randy pulled away in shock. He hadn't expected Rebecca to kiss him. She had hesitated for a second, pulling back only to change her mind. Was she thinking of Alistair? If she gave him a chance, Randy knew that he could make Rebecca Valencourt forget about the twin. He knew Alistair had broken her heart. Courage flooded into him. He had made it this far, and he would fight for her, even if she was still fighting against herself and her own desire for Alistair. Without hesitating, he pulled her close and crushed his lips against hers. He could feel her smiling against his mouth. His hands moved across her back, and tangled in her hair, pulling her closer still.

The song changed by the time their kiss ended. Randy didn't need to look around to know people were staring at them. Rebecca took his hand and led him toward one of the darkened hallways. He glanced up just long enough to see Tennille's proud face and Laila's giddy expression. He grinned and turned to see Rebecca's curly brown hair. He couldn't wait to get his fingers back in it.

CHAPTER NINETEEN

Alistair wandered the party alone. He didn't want to see any of his friends, just Rebecca. He needed to tell her that he had been accepted to Harvard. Sterling's excitement had been tempered with disappointment. They would be going to different schools next year, the first time in eighteen years the brothers would be apart. Alistair knew his parents were not going to be happy with Harvard but damn all of their traditions.

He looked around the basement, searching for Rebecca's curly brown locks. She would be thrilled; she would be supportive. But she was nowhere to be found. Spotting what appeared to be a drugged out, belligerent Kalyn and a moderately intoxicated Tasha, Alistair made his way over to them, hoping they knew where he could find Rebecca.

"Hey, Alistair!" Kalyn threw her arms around him, spilling her drink down his back.

"Hi, Kalyn," Alistair said, trying to feign interest at seeing her. He hated what she had done to Sterling and her supercilious attitude and malicious behavior only deepened his dislike.

"You might want to lay off those pills, especially when you drink."

"So caring," Kalyn crooned, tousling his hair. "Not like your brother."

"Have you two seen Rebecca tonight?" Alistair asked, peeling the drunken blonde from his chest and resting her against a wall. Kalyn looked hopeless but Tasha appeared somewhat coherent.

Tasha gave him a pitiful look and Kalyn answered his question with a shrill laugh. "Rebecca," Kalyn said, bracing herself against a chair, "left half an hour ago with Randy."

"What?" Alistair's head snapped around to face her.

"Randy Showman," Kalyn laughed again.

Alistair could see Tasha rolling her eyes. "Rebecca's been acting like such a little bitch for the past few months and earlier today she got her panties all in a bunch over something. Now she's probably off fucking Randy Showman."

Kalyn chuckled.

Alistair didn't find anything amusing.

"Where did they go?" He clenched his fists in anger.

"That way," Kalyn pointed down a hallway and Alistair was off. He dreaded finding Rebecca. The hallway led to storage closets, abandoned classrooms, and an old swimming pool. He imagined Randy Showman coolly pushing Rebecca up against one of the walls, kissing her full lips, his hands roving on top of her shirt and caressing her breasts.

Quiet laughter echoed down the hallway and he quickened his pace, his fists clenched. A hand on his arm grabbed him and he spun around.

"What?" Tasha stood beside him.

"Alistair, maybe you should leave her alone."

"You wouldn't understand," he protested, trying to shrug her hand away.

"She looked really happy," Tasha said quickly. "Happier than I've seen her in a long time."

That stopped him. He hadn't seen Rebecca look happy all year and he worried that she would hurt herself.

"Shit," he swore, putting a hand on Tasha's shoulder.

Tasha flashed a sympathetic smile. "Come have a drink with me. We can talk about it."

He had always liked Tasha's blunt comments and her confidence. When Sterling and Kalyn had been together, they had grown quiet close. She had always been a confidant, someone besides Sterling whom Alistair could talk to.

"I don't want to stay here. Can we go somewhere else?"

Tasha grinned. "Of course. There's a bottle of Bulleit in my room."

Of course she would have the good stuff. Tasha was the only girl he knew who could handle bourbon.

129

"Is Kalyn going to be there?" he asked, hesitant to include his brother's ex-girlfriend in anything.

Tasha shook her head. "No. She stocked up on pills and alcohol to last her through the night, so I doubt I'll see her until tomorrow afternoon."

Alistair followed her up to the room, the hallways deserted, and the rooms quiet. Tasha opened the door and walked inside, her light brown hair hanging straight to her shoulders, her hips swaying slightly more than usual in her inebriated state. Alistair looked at her as she opened her drawer and produced the bottle. She wasn't what he would call pretty. Her hair was constantly in her face, her features slightly small and mouse-like, but she looked honest and wholesome – more than he could say for 90% of the girls at Harper's.

"I don't have any glasses," Tasha said, sitting on her bed and opening the bottle. "We'll have to drink it straight."

"I don't mind," Alistair smiled and sat next to her. She took a large gulp, closing her eyes and enjoying the warmth of the liquor. She passed him the bottle and stared at him.

"So, talk. I don't think I've seen you this upset before."

"It's just the alcohol. I'll get over it in the morning."

"Liar."

Alistair smiled. Tasha could read anyone, see through everyone's bullshit.

"All right," he finally conceded. "Randy Showman?"

Tasha took the bottle from his hand, taking another sip before setting it on her nightstand.

"Randy Showman," she confirmed. "Not really something anyone expected."

"She's never been with another guy. I guess I imagined she would always just be with me."

"And you really thought that would last even though you refused to make her your girlfriend?"

"It lasted this long," Alistair pointed out.

"Right, and now she has finally realized there is someone else besides the amazing Alistair Pierce. It had to happen one day."

"I know, it did." Alistair reached for the bottle and drank two long, full swigs.

"So why are you so upset?"

"I guess I didn't realize what I had until it was gone."

"Classic."

"I don't know, lately I've been missing her, you know? She hasn't been around as much and I've been feeling as though something isn't complete."

"Alistair, look. I know that you like her in your own way, but it's not fair for you to string her along just because you like having sex with her. Rebecca's a really nice girl and deserves more than that."

"I know she does." He had been an ass to her the last three years.

"The girl is finally growing some balls and if you cared about her at all, you would let her go."

"It hurts, Tasha," he said quietly.

"She's been hurting a lot longer than you have," Tasha snapped.

"I really fucked up with her, didn't I?"

"Probably," Tasha stated confidently. "For a while at least."

"You think she would take me back, eventually?"

"If you were willing to commit, maybe."

Alistair sighed. He wanted to commit, but he couldn't. He wasn't like Sterling. The thought of being with one girl made him feel claustrophobic, constricted. He was only eighteen.

"Tasha, you're the best. Has anyone ever told you that?"

"I tell myself that every morning, as a matter of fact."

Alistair stood up from the bed, taking one last swig from the bottle.

"How is your brother doing?"

He frowned as he put the bottle down. "Sterling? He's fine, I guess."

"It's really too bad what happened. But Kalyn's taken the morning after pill multiple times and she says it's just like getting really bad period cramps for a few hours."

"What the hell are you talking about?"

"Didn't he tell you?" Tasha looked up at him.

"Tell me what?"

"Jenna found Laila's prescription for the morning after pill."

What did she just say? Sterling wasn't one to share the intimate details of his sex life with Alistair, but he was pretty sure he would have informed his brother if he and Laila had been sleeping together.

"That's impossible. Laila and Sterling aren't having sex."

"Oh," Tasha said, looking as though just the thought of having sex made her uncomfortable. "Maybe you should talk to him about it then? Maybe he doesn't know."

"He would have told me if he did." He had to find his brother.

There was a short silence and Tasha looked as if she had more to say.

"Do you know something else?" Alistair asked impatiently.

"I probably shouldn't mention it, but Kalyn seems to think that Laila and Chase might be doing more than studying in the library."

"What?" h asked, feeling drunk.

"Apparently they spend the entire time flirting and whispering. And then they leave together."

"That doesn't mean anything."

"It's all gossip, I know. But it has to come from somewhere."

Alistair nodded his head in agreement and thought about what he had seen between Laila and Chase. They were friendly, but not overly so. He had dismissed it before. Maybe Chase and Laila were hiding something, but she really didn't seem the type to cheat on anyone.

"Thank you for the booze and the honesty, Tasha. Both are appreciated," Alistair said, wanting to find his brother as soon as possible.

"Any time. You know that, right?" Tasha walked him to the door.

"I do. And please let me know if I can ever return the favor. I know I'm not the best at advice, but I can at least buy you a bottle of bourbon." He gave her a big hug and a kiss on the cheek.

The door closed softly behind him and clicked locked. He passed by Rebecca's door and wondered where she was and what she was doing. The thought of who she might be doing nearly made him gag.

CHAPTER TWENTY

$\mathcal{O}$pening his browser, Sterling searched for Plan B medication and clicked on the first result. The morning after pill. But why would she need that? He searched for other common uses for the medication but found none. Had Laila deceived him? Had she lied to him and cheated on him? No, that couldn't be possible.

He had been on his way to meet Laila at the party when Trace Albertson had offered his advice about unwanted pregnancies. At first, Sterling couldn't figure out why Trace would talk about pregnancy. He had to ask his friend to repeat himself multiple times before he finally told Sterling about the prescription. Apparently the school knew – except him.

Stunned, Sterling had run to Jenna Frank's room and demanded she turn the paper over to him. The poor girl looked about to cry but gave it willingly and Sterling's heart sank like an anvil in water at the sight of Laila's name.

He slammed the screen shut and pushed away from his desk, glaring at the paper lying next to his computer. It couldn't be. Quickly, he grabbed his phone and dialed her number, the call going straight to voicemail. She must have been at the party.

"Fuck!" he screamed as he ended the call. He knew that he should give her the benefit of the doubt and wait until she came to his room so they could talk about it. But as he paced in front of his door, he felt his anger growing and knew he would need to talk to her before it got out of control. He didn't want to scare her off but he would only get angrier the longer he waited. He needed to find her, have a quick conversation, and then laugh about it later. Digging through his clothes, he found a pair of jeans and a sweatshirt and was nearly out the door when Alistair came in looking horrific. Great night all around. He must have looked even worse because Alistair perked up a bit.

"Oh, no. Did you hear?" His brother asked, looking him up and down.

"Hear about what?" Sterling asked through clenched teeth.

The silence lingered for a moment too long and Sterling shook his head and pushed past his brother.

"I need to find Laila," he grumbled but Alistair stopped him.

"Don't go yet," his brother pleaded and grabbed for his arm. "We should talk about this."

"Talk about what, Alistair? She went to the nurse two days ago and got a prescription for this."

Sterling grabbed the paper from his desk and shoved it in his brother's face. "We haven't had sex yet so why the hell would she need it?"

"Fuck, man. I don't know what to say,"

"I don't want to believe she would do this to me. I have to go find her."

Alistair's hand went to the back of his neck and he looked around uncomfortably. "Look, it's hard for me to tell you this because I can see how much you like her, but there are rumors going around that Laila is doing more with Chase then just helping him with physics."

"What?" Sterling shouted.

"People are saying that all they do is flirt and whisper," he took a deep breath before finishing. "And then they leave together."

"I'll fucking kill them both!"

Sterling turned away from his brother and stormed out the door.

"Sterling, wait! Don't do anything stupid!" he heard his brother call from behind him. Sterling ran down the hallway and out into the cold December air. He reached Wellsworth Hall and sprinted down the stairs, two at a time. Couples danced in the flashes of the strobe light.

And there she was. Laila, his Laila, in the arms of none other than Chase Nichols, her face flushed, a smile on her mouth. She threw her head back and laughed at something.

He shuddered and a deep rage filled his body.

CHAPTER TWENTY-ONE

Tennille chided her dancing yet again but Laila only laughed. She had a hard time taking the instruction very seriously. She just wanted to have fun and knew she would never be a pro at it.

The girls were waiting for Tate and Sterling to arrive but the more they drank and the later it got, the more restless they became. Tenille wanted to dance so Laila had reluctantly accompanied her onto the floor.

"Laila! Listen to me," Tennille said, holding Laila's hand in a tight grip.

"You know what?" Laila replied as she noticed Tate approaching them. "I think I'll sit this one out."

Tennille glanced over her shoulder and dropped Laila's hand when she saw her boyfriend approach.

"I just have to say," Tate glanced between the girls before sweeping Tennille into his arms, "watching you two dance has been the highlight of my night."

Laila laughed but Tennille whispered something in his ear. His eyes grew larger and his hands held her tightly to his body.

Laila knew when she was no longer wanted. "Have a good night." Tennille gave her a wink.

Laila found an empty chair and sat down, rather exhausted from Tennille's dance lessons. She turned and caught a group of five girls all staring at her. They turned quickly away and formed a circle. What was going on? Did someone know something she didn't? She felt like the butt of a joke. Feeling increasingly uncomfortable, she wondered what was taking Sterling so long.

"Can I have this dance?" she heard from behind her.

"Chase," she said, standing up. She had been pleasantly surprised by him during their months of tutoring. He had been a gentleman and although she never would have expected it, they had developed a friendship.

"I shouldn't," she told him. "I'm waiting for Sterling."

"And he's not here yet. Come on, consider it a tutor, tuteree dance. It's harmless."

"Okay."

He lightly held her hand and brought her out onto the dance floor. The music played slow and soft and Laila felt a bit uncomfortable, the mood more intimate than she wanted.

"Have you gotten into any colleges yet?" she asked to break the uncomfortable silence.

"Not any good ones," Chase admitted, grinning sheepishly.

"But your physics grade has to be improving."

"It is, thanks to you."

"I do what I can," Laila said with a smile.

"And I appreciate all your efforts. And so do my parents. Buying my good grades was starting to cost them a fortune," he deadpanned.

Laila couldn't help but laugh at the casual way Chase talked about his cheating. She didn't approve but admired his devil-may-care attitude. Not many could pull it off without sounding like a complete jerk but Chase managed to make it charming somehow.

"Well, I am happy to help in your rehabilitation."

"Does that mean you are finally going to let me take you out?" Chase spun her around as Laila blushed. He had been asking her out for weeks now and she had been refusing. He had claimed it was only a friendly date, a thank you for all the hours she had spent tutoring him. Chase had the potential to make some girl incredibly happy, but she wasn't the one. She was so deeply in love with Sterling, she couldn't think straight half the time.

"No. It means that I will continue to tutor you though."

"I guess I'll take what I can get," he said with a grin. His smile turned into a frown. Laila followed his gaze and saw Sterling standing a few feet away from them, his face red and his fists clenched.

"Hey," she said, happy to see him. "There you are. I've been waiting all night."

Sterling glared like a feral cat, his eyes mere slits, his lips pulled into a tight line, his chest heaving.

"Sterling? Are you all right?"

"No," he snapped at her. "No, Laila, I'm not all right."

"What's wrong?"

"I'm guessing you know what's wrong."

Laila wanted to laugh. She had never seen him like this before and she didn't know if she should be amused or scared. "Okay, well, I don't so…"

"Did you think I would never find out? Did you think that I wouldn't notice? The whole school is talking about it Laila and I am apparently the last one to know."

"Notice what? What are they talking about?" Sterling wasn't making any sense.

"Did you think I wouldn't notice that you weren't really a virgin?"

"What the hell are you talking about?" Laila pushed out of Chase's arms and took a hesitant step toward Sterling. He looked rabid. What had happened?

"I'm talking about you cheating on me with Chase."

"Will you keep your voice down?" Laila snapped at him once she realized the music had stopped and people were starting to stare at her again. "Look, if this is a joke, it's not funny."

"Does it look like I'm joking?" Sterling crossed his arms and glared down at her as she moved closer to him.

"You think Chase and I are sleeping together?"

"I know you are."

Laila turned around and looked at Chase, hoping to find some help. Chase started walking toward them.

"Why would you think that?" She was trying to stay as calm as possible.

"People are talking about it. Everyone is talking about it. I have proof."

Laila realized that everyone had been staring at her because of some rumor. Although she had tried to avoid it from day one, her reputation had been dragged through the mud.

"And you believed them? You know how people gossip here and you know that none of it is true."

"So you're denying it?"

"Yes! Of course I am denying it!"

"Can I just say something?" Chase said. "Laila's a great girl and I really like her but I can honestly say that we have never slept together. She won't even let me take her out for coffee." His hand rested protectively on her shoulder.

"Don't touch her," Sterling hissed. "Why him? Of all people." Sterling demanded, pointing at the lanky kid. "Why pretend you want to wait and make it special when you're sleeping with him?"

"Damn-it! We are not sleeping together!" Laila no longer cared that they were causing a scene.

"Then how do you explain this?" Sterling reached into his pocket and produced the prescription.

"What is this?" Laila took it from his hand and examined it.

"It's a prescription for Plan B. Someone found it in the bathroom."

"This isn't mine," Laila said, looking down at the paper which did indeed have her name scribbled across the top. How could that be? She searched her memory and was certain that she had never seen the paper before. That could only mean one thing. Forgery of a medical document. Wasn't that a felony? Not that it mattered to anyone at Harper's; their parents could simply pay to have any crime wiped clean. "I don't even know what this is."

"Plan B? That's the morning after pill," Chase said, reading over her shoulder.

Sterling lunged for him but Chase stepped out of the way.

"Who gave this to you?" Laila demanded, stepping between the two to prevent a fight.

"What does it matter?"

"I guess it doesn't." Laila no longer felt confused, just anger and sadness. "If you don't want to believe me, that's your problem. But you know me better than this. I can't play the games that you play here, Sterling. It's not who I am and I could never be the kind of girl who acts a certain way with one boy and a completely different way with another. I wouldn't even know how to carry on an affair and why would I be stupid enough to try it here at Harper's where every student knows everyone else's business?"

He seemed to consider what she had said but didn't change his mind. "Everyone knows about you two, Laila. You leave the library together every Thursday."

"I don't care what everyone says, Sterling. He walks me back to the dorms because it's dark. He's trying to be a gentleman, something you used to be."

"Laila," Sterling's voice shook with anger and uncertainty. "I want to believe you, but this is too much to ignore," he said, taking the prescription back from her.

Laila felt the pressure building in her head, anger: hurt, and sadness mixing and expanding to fill her whole body. How could Sterling believe this about her? She thought they were on the same page. Like steam from a boiling kettle, Laila's anger grew. She gritted her teeth and spoke softly but firmly. "You may not believe me when I tell you I have never slept with Chase but I hope you believe me when I tell you that I will never sleep with you either, so I guess you'll never know for sure."

She could see something shift in Sterling's eyes – maybe the realization he had gone too far and let his anger get ahead of him. Too bad. He was a fucking asshole. He caught her arm as she pushed past him, trying to make a quick exit from the building. "Laila, I'm sorry."

"Save it for someone who cares, Sterling," she said bitterly, avoiding eye contact.

"Can you give me just a few minutes so we can talk about this?"

"No. Now let go of me." She couldn't understand how one minute he could be so furious and the next be so calm about the scene he had just made.

"Please, can you hear me out?"

Laila glared at him with all the rage she could muster. But the words had released the pressure and the anger with it. Now, she felt only heartbroken.

"No, Sterling. Let me go."

Reluctantly, Sterling's hand left her arm and she fled the room, running through the cold air of campus. She ran to the edge of the woods and then walked across a soccer field, staring at the stars in the sky. The moon illuminated plumes of her breath as she sobbed. What was she doing at Harper's? She didn't fit in. She didn't get picked on and ridiculed like Randy but the isolation she felt was just as great. Sterling had made it better and now even he turned out to be like all the rest of them. She didn't know what she had done to deserve this. Didn't know what she had done to make him believe that she would ever sleep with another man. But Sterling had believed it. She had seen it in his eyes.

She began walking back towards Widden Hall. It would be so easy to bail. She wiped the tears from her face and picked up the pace. They weren't going to drive her out. Whoever had started the rumor could go to hell. She came here to get into Yale and that's what she was going to do. "When the going gets tough, the tough get going," her grandfather had always said.

145

And she wasn't going to be corrupted or changed by this place. She liked who she was and had no intention of becoming a "Harper's girl": a bottle in one hand, a pocket book in the other, and flat on your back.

She walked into her room, surprising Tennille and Tate who were half undressed. That might as well be the uniform for this place. They could tattoo the damn crest on everyone's bare chest. She grabbed her inhaler out of her bag, taking two doses and closing her eyes until the medicine had worked its magic.

"Laila? Laila, what happened to you?"

Laila took a deep breath and turned to Tennille. "I think it's over between me and Sterling," she said, falling onto her bed and collapsing into sobs.

CHAPTER TWENTY-TWO

Sterling pushed his way through the door of his English class. Today the door felt as if it weighed two thousand pounds. It was the last day of classes before winter break and he should have been thrilled. He should have woken up with Laila in his arms, told her how much he was looking forward to visiting her in California, and told her how much he was going to miss her until then. But instead, he had spent the better part of the night outside her room, pleading with her through the door to let him in. All he needed to do was explain his actions, then she would give him a second chance.

But eventually Tennille had come out, reasoned with him that Laila wasn't in any condition to speak with him, and asked him to kindly leave before she called campus security. He had caught a quick view of Laila as Tennille had walked back through the door. She had been curled up on her bed, crying, her thin shoulders and arms hugging her legs tight to her chest. The sight nearly broke Sterling and he didn't think he would survive the night knowing he had caused her so much pain. He tossed and turned, waking up every fifteen minutes with tears in his eyes or his fists clenched in rage.

He knew Laila would be in class and part of him wanted to see her while another part of him wanted to run away. Maybe she had forgiven him. Maybe he could finally talk to her. But perhaps she was still angry. Perhaps she would ignore him, treat him like the bastard he really was.

He walked through the door and saw her beautiful face first. She sat in the front row, far from their normal spot. Their eyes met for a brief moment before she turned quickly away. The bell rang. He walked towards her as the other students sat down.

"Can I talk to you?" He stood in front of her chair and stared down at her.

"No," she whispered, not looking at him.

"You need to understand how sorry I am." He didn't care that Chuck Kelleher and Lilly Hirschfeld were listening and watching. Word of their fight had spread like wildfire through the school. Apparently there was even a Facebook group dedicated to dissecting the breakup.

"I don't care," Laila lied and they both knew it. Tears swelled in her lids.

Sterling opened his mouth to speak but was interrupted by the professor. "Mr. Pierce, would you care to take your seat?"

Sterling walked to his seat, his eyes never leaving Laila. The seat next to him, her seat, remained empty.

"All right, since this is the last day of the semester, I assume you have all completed the reading." Some of the students nodded in affirmation and others fidgeted.

"Would anyone care to share their opinion on it?"

No one raised a hand and the class remained silent.

"Mr. Pierce?" The teacher's voice lifted Sterling's gaze from Laila's back. "Perhaps that question was too broad. Would you like to explain who you felt was the most tragic character in Shakespeare's play?"

Sterling cleared his throat. "The title character, Othello."

"Please, elaborate."

"He killed his wife after being led to believe something that wasn't true and then, in all his misery and guilt, he kills himself. That's pretty tragic."

The professor looked around the room at the blank faces of the students. "Miss Roberts, you're shaking your head. Do you not agree with Mr. Pierce?"

Laila sat up straight in her chair. "Othello's tragedy doesn't come from the fact that he killed himself or Desdemona. He is a tragic character because he allowed his pride to overshadow his love."

"Continue." The professor flashed an encouraging smile.

"In the first act, when he is accused of witchcraft, he uses his charm and his honesty to discredit those claims, proving himself to those who accuse him and winning their affection. But when his wife's fidelity

149

is questioned, he chooses to believe Iago and his less-than-credible evidence above his wife's word because the rumors have hurt his ego. He kills her, forgetting he was once in her situation, accused of something that wasn't true. His pride interferes with everything he has worked so hard to accomplish, thus ultimately leading to his downfall. That is the real tragedy."

"Well said, now..."

Sterling interrupted the professor, "But maybe someone before Desdemona hurt Othello so badly that he couldn't help but feel betrayed. Maybe Othello has trust issues."

Some of the kids in the class giggled at his desperate attempt at a rebuttal.

"Then maybe Othello should learn to separate the present from the past. Maybe Othello shouldn't jump to conclusions." Laila crossed her arms but didn't turn around.

"But he loves Desdemona so much," Sterling said, practically pleading for Laila to turn around and look at him. "He loves her so much that he can't see reason. He loves her so much, he's scared of getting hurt."

Laila finally looked at him The rest of the class stared at her, waiting for a response. She didn't say a word. Her lips trembled and a soft pink blush colored her cheeks.

"I think we're getting off topic," the teacher said, trying to regain the attention of the class. "Who wants to share their notes on the theme of racism in this story?"

Sterling didn't hear him. He stared at the beautiful girl who sat trembling in the front row.

"I love you."

Laila bit her lip and blinked rapidly.

"I'm sorry," he mouthed next and she finally gave him a tiny smile. She turned back around. Maybe it would be okay.

 CHAPTER TWENTY-THREE

Sterling's mind raced as he bounded down the stairs after the bell had rung. Dashing outside, he grabbed Laila's hand and pulled her down the hallway into an empty classroom. Once inside, with the door shut, he shed his backpack and pulled her into his arms. He felt her hesitate but she didn't pull away. She didn't say a word. They remained silent until the second bell had sounded, reminding everyone they should be in their next class.

"Laila," Sterling eventually said, pulling back and kissing the top of her head. "I'm so sorry. Please, please forgive me."

His hands ran up and down her arms and back. Her shoulders curled into him and her chest pressed against his.

"You scared me so much last night, Sterling," she said, her voice trembling.

"I know and I'm so sorry. There's really no excuse for what I did." His hands went to the back of

152

her head, combed through her hair and glided over the smooth skin on her neck.

"Can you try to explain? Because I really don't understand what happened."

"I'll try." His fingers traced her cheek and her jaw as his other hand slid back down to her waist, moving slowly between her ribs and her hip. "I thought after last night I'd never get to touch you again," he said quietly. "The thought nearly killed me."

She managed a weak smile. Sterling knew he was lucky she was allowing him to touch her at all. He didn't exactly know where to start. He had tried to avoid the memories as much as possible.

"I know we've never talked about this, but I thought you may have heard it from someone else." He took a deep breath. "Kalyn Andretti and I used to be a couple. We were together for a little less than a year."

Laila looked stunned. Clearly no one had told her and Sterling swallowed the lump in his throat, knowing his explanation had just become that much harder.

"Kalyn? You and Kalyn?" Laila took a step back from him, but his hands remained on her shoulders.

"I know," Sterling smiled at her response, hoping to soothe the shock. "It seems impossible, I know, but she was a different person back then. She wasn't as heartless and cold as she is now."

"Why didn't you ever tell me? Why didn't anyone else tell me?"

"It didn't end well. I'm guessing no one told you about it because of what it did to me."

"What did it do to you?" Laila put her hands on her hips.

"It crushed me. She left me, completely out of the blue, saying she had fallen for Julian Polk. I knew they were family friends but they never seemed to be anything more than that. She gave no other explanation. She refused to speak to me, refused to answer any of my questions. It wasn't until months and months later that everyone learned about their arranged engagement."

Laila's body relaxed a bit. Sterling didn't explain that Kalyn still had feelings for him and that his ex wanted to get back together. Undoubtedly, that explained the animosity she had towards Laila. Laila already knew. "You know that she still has feelings for you, right?"

"I know that. And I also know that what happened between us left me with a lot of baggage. When I heard the rumors about you and Chase, I felt betrayed all over again. I should have come to you first but then I saw Alistair. What he told me about you and Chase in the library just confirmed my worst fears. I just snapped."

"It was all hearsay, Sterling. I can't believe you would trust that over me!"

"I know, I know. I am completely in the wrong here. It's just that my feelings for you are so strong, stronger than anything I've ever felt before. It scares me to think how much you could hurt me if you wanted to."

Laila paused for only a moment, a frown on her face. "What makes you think I ever would?" she asked, her voice now light and inquisitive.

"Nothing. Nothing you have done has ever made me think you would hurt me. But when I was with Kalyn, nothing she ever did gave me that impression either."

"I'm not her, Sterling."

"I know you aren't," he said, taking a step toward her and causing her to back against the wall. "And I will never doubt you again. I promise."

He reached for her and when she didn't shy away from him, he knew she had made up her mind to forgive him. The guilt wouldn't subside for days, maybe weeks, but at least he would have her, his perfect Laila.

"I've apologized to Chase," he whispered as he pulled her to his chest again. "And I'll do anything to make this up to you. I love you so much."

Laila didn't respond right away but that didn't bother him. He could feel her nuzzling her face in his chest, adjusting her arms around his waist so she could pull him as tight as he could possibly go.

"I love you, too," she finally whispered, looking up at him. "I hate myself for forgiving you so easily. But don't do this again." He nodded. "Next time I won't forgive."

"You really love me, too?"

She nodded slowly but confidently.

Sterling sighed in relief. "I should have told you the second I realized I was in love with you," he whispered.

"And when was that?" Laila asked, her expression playful and inquisitive.

"Probably that morning I woke up in Tennille's bed and your face was the first thing I saw. I wrote you that note telling you how I couldn't wait to see you again," Sterling admitted, slightly embarrassed by his confession though not wanting to hold anything back. "I've wanted to say it for such a long time now."

Laila blushed.

His hands cupped her face as he bent down to kiss her. Her lips, her breath, the soft noises she made when he kissed her, everything was perfect. He loved everything about her. He couldn't get enough. His lips left her mouth and traveled down her jaw to her neck. His hands wandered as well, leaving her face and finding their way to other parts of her body.

"Sterling, stop," he heard Laila giggle as she pushed him away. "We're in a classroom."

"Sorry," he grinned devilishly, making her blush. "I just hated waking up without you this morning. I need to make up for lost time."

"You've woken up without me plenty of mornings."

"I know. But last night was our only night together for a while and I wanted to spend it with you."

"Well, I didn't sleep much last night and I'm pretty tired. I could use a nap, if you're interested."

"A nap sounds perfect," he whispered and bent down to kiss her again.

"But just a nap, understand?" she said, pushing him away. "I'm still angry at you."

Sterling smiled at her determined face. "Whatever you say."

"Okay, good," she said, taking his hand and leading him out of the classroom.

Nearly six inches of fresh snow had fallen in the middle of the night, making the campus look like a fairy world. Snow capped the statues and made the stone and brick buildings look almost like gingerbread. On the main quad, a couple of freshman threw snowballs at each other.

Laila wrapped her arm around Sterling to keep from slipping, her eyes wide in wonder.

"This is your first time seeing snow, isn't it?" Sterling asked, amused at her reaction to it.

"I've been skiing before," she informed him.

"That's not the same thing."

"No, it's not." She smiled and sighed, looking around the campus. Sterling pulled away and grabbed a handful of snow, playfully tossing it at her.

"Sterling!"

She bent down, picked up a handful of snow, and returned the favor. It hit him square in the shoulder. She giggled at his look of playful surprise.

"Did you just throw a snowball at me?"

"You threw one at me," she laughed.

"You're going to pay for that." he bent down and scooped up another handful.

Laila squealed and took off running, Sterling's footsteps crunching behind her. He closed the distance quickly and grabbed her waist, picking her up and swinging Laila into his arms. She laughed in delight as he carried her across the white lawn to the dormitories.

CHAPTER TWENTY-FOUR

"What the hell happened at the party last night?" Kalyn asked, storming into Chase's room without knocking.

"You were there. Didn't you see it?" Chase knew what she was referring to because the entire school was talking about it.

Kalyn scoffed. "I don't remember much of last night."

Chase rolled his eyes, knowing she had taken one too many pills or had one too many drinks. "You've probably heard it all. Laila and I were dancing and Sterling came over and accused her of sleeping with me and not being a virgin. They argued and she left."

"Then what?"

"Then nothing. Sterling followed her and I drank some more."

Kalyn looked pissed and Chase couldn't understand why. Didn't she want that to happen? Laila and Sterling were on the outs and everyone knew that Kalyn still had feelings for him.

"They made up during first period," she finally sighed and Chase nodded his head. He knew that they would. Sterling might not be able to control his temper, but he wasn't an idiot. Letting go of someone as great as Laila would have been the worst mistake the guy could have made.

"You know, you could have helped the situation," Kalyn snapped at him.

"I did help. I told him that Laila and I had never slept together."

Kalyn's mouth dropped open and she looked about ready to erupt. Mount Kalyn, Chase chuckled to himself.

"*Our* situation, Chase. You could have helped *our* situation."

"I'm not following you," he told her, crossing his arms in front of his chest.

"What you should have done is kept your mouth shut until Laila left and then told Sterling some story about how she threw herself at you."

Chase pondered her suggestion and realized that it could have worked to his benefit.

"You've ruined everything," Kalyn told him before he could reply.

"And what exactly have I ruined? My chances with Laila? Those were ruined the second she met Sterling."

"Don't be so selfish," Kalyn scolded him. "There was more at stake than your fairy-tale ending with the California princess."

"Oh, are you referring to your ridiculous dream of seducing Sterling Pierce?"

"So what if I am? He loved me once and he could easily be persuaded to love me again."

"Don't you get it?" Chase said. "Sterling is done with you. You'll never get him back. It's over. Move on. And as for me and Laila, she's never going to fall for me. She is completely obsessed with him. Obsessed in a completely non-stalkerish way, just the opposite of your obsession."

"Maybe you just didn't try hard enough," Kalyn said, looking away, unwilling to listen to the truth.

"Like you have?"

"Okay, Chase. Listen to me," she said, trying to bring the focus back to what he wanted. "Do you still want to be with Laila?"

"I think maybe it's time I let it go. I know she's happy with him and it's not worth the effort to get in the way of that," Chase said, digging deep to find that much compassion for another human being.

"What if I told you that there was a way we could get Sterling and Laila to break up with each other with only minimal effort on your part?"

Chase considered it and ultimately shrugged his shoulders. "I guess I would want to hear what you had in mind."

"Good," Kalyn said with a victorious smile. "Because we'll need to work together on this."

"Because we work together so well, don't we?"

"Do you want to hear my plan or not?"

161

"I don't know. All this arguing is getting me a little worked up," Chase said with a devious smile.

"I can get Laila to break up with Sterling. He already has a tiny bit of doubt from the whole Plan B situation. But you need to do everything I say."

"Did you forge that prescription?" Chase asked and Kalyn looked appalled.

"That's a horrible thing to accuse someone of. Now shut up and listen."

"You know I don't like being told what to do." Chase pulled his shirt over his head and threw it on the bed.

"I know you don't. But you could live with it, for Laila." Kalyn kicked off her shoes and lowered her stockings, knowing that Chase wasn't going to listen to anything she had to say until he had been physically satisfied.

"Do you already have a plan?" Chase's eyes followed Kalyn's hand as she ran it down her chest and across her stomach.

"Don't I always?" she said softly as she let her skirt fall around her ankles.

CHAPTER TWENTY-FIVE

Julian knocked on Kalyn's door. The semester was over and they were scheduled to meet their parents at Boston's Logan airport in less than two hours. The six of them would be vacationing in St. Tropez, like they did every year. The two families shared a house, dined together, and had the same political discussions year after year. He couldn't believe that at eighteen he was already finding his life repetitious and mundane.

"Julian, hi." Tasha opened the door with a smile.

Tasha's grey eyes looked particularly pretty. "Hey, Tasha. Is Kalyn in there? I'm ready to go."

"She's not here," Tasha said, opening the door wider so he could see for himself. "I don't know where she is."

Julian swore under his breath. If she made them miss their flight, he would be beyond angry. "Can I come in and get her bags? I can at least take them to the car while I wait for her."

"I don't think she's packed yet. Why don't you come in?"

Julian stepped into the room. Tasha had made her bed, her Louis Vuitton suitcases neatly lined up next to her dresser. It looked like a hurricane had hit Kalyn's side of the room. Clothes were strewn across her bed and on the floor, luggage open and empty on the floor. Shoes and purses overflowed the closet.

"Christ, do I have to do everything for her?" Julian made his way over to her bed and started throwing items into her suitcase. Tasha didn't say a word and folded her laptop into the case before slipping it into a duffel bag.

"Are you going to France this winter?" Julian had spent one pleasant evening in St. Tropez last winter. The Davenports had a home in Cannes and had driven over to spend the weekend with the Andrettis. Tasha had surprised him that evening. She had been able to hold her own in an adult conversation, unlike Kalyn who looked bored around any discussion that didn't involve clothes or shopping. Tasha's poise had left a lasting impression on Julian.

"No," Tasha said, much to his disappointment. "This year we're going to Belize."

"Are you leaving from Boston? I could give you a ride..."

"I'm catching the train back to Vermont. We're leaving on Monday."

Julian moved to Kalyn's underwear drawer and emptied the contents into the bag. She could sort through it when she got to France. *If* she got to France. Her tardiness was going to ruin his entire...but wait. If they did miss their flight, certainly their parents would go without them. They had obligations: dinners, lunches, cocktail parties. Julian would be free to do whatever he wanted for the entire vacation: walk around the house naked, invite over as many girls as he pleased, throw parties and drink his parents' expensive bourbon.

"Well, if Kalyn doesn't show up soon, we may be joining you in Vermont."

"Don't look so happy about it. I'm sure there is more than one flight to Paris."

"Can I ask you a question?" Tasha had always been the cool, pragmatic one, the voice of reason.

Tasha checked her watch and then smiled at him. "Sure. My driver won't be here for another half hour."

"You know Kalyn pretty well, right?"

"As well as anyone would want to know her, I suppose."

Julian smiled. Tasha really never held anything back. "Do you think it's worth it? I mean, do you think that risking my inheritance is worth marrying someone I don't love?"

"Well," Tasha sat down on her bed, clearly prepared for a lengthy discussion. Julian couldn't help but notice the way she casually crossed her legs under her black skirt. Her thick and textured tights hugged the strong muscles of her thighs. She sat up straight, her stomach and chest nearly as flat as her back. Tasha wasn't as attractive as Kalyn but she had an understated beauty which he was growing to appreciate.

165

"I think that you need to consider what you value more, love or money," she told him.

"If I said money, would you think less of me?"

Tasha laughed. "No. It's honest and it's your choice."

Julian sighed. "But that's not my answer."

"You value love more than money? Are you sure you aren't confusing love with sex?"

"I'm sure. I've had enough sex to last a lifetime, probably. But falling in love isn't as easy as having sex. Hell, it isn't as easy as spending money, either. I know that when I do fall in love, it will be forever."

"You just have to find the right girl, right?"

"Exactly. I'm afraid, though, that I'll find her once it's too late. I'll find her right after I marry Kalyn. We'll be thrown into some hot affair and things will end badly once my wife finds out."

"That's a rather tragic story. Very Shakespearian."

"What about you? Would you marry for money?"

"Me? Not in a million years!" Tasha said with a laugh, as if the entire idea was preposterous. "But, then again, my parents aren't threatening to take away my inheritance."

"It's not really fair, you know? Being thrown into something like this. I mean, we didn't have a say in the matter. I could take it if she hadn't turned into such a raging bitch over the last year."

"Careful now. That's your fiancée you're talking about. You might want to be a little nicer unless you want your life to be a complete hell."

"I can't help it," Julian laughed with her. "She's psychotic!"

"Who's psychotic?" Kalyn stood in the doorway, her hair tangled and her face flushed. Julian didn't even have to guess what she had been doing and he really didn't give a damn who she had been doing it with.

"Professor Norton," he replied, looking completely at ease lying.

Kalyn rolled her eyes. "Fucking bitch tried to fail me last year."

"I packed for you. Let's go."

Kalyn's face darkened. "Why would you do that? You couldn't possibly know what I need or which accessories--" Julian interrupted her to head off a long tirade.

"I did it because you failed to do it yourself. I'm not missing the plane because you're too lazy to pack a suitcase."

"Well, I'm leaving. You two have fun in France," Tasha said with a cheery grin. She passed Kalyn and then gave Julian a wink before walking out the door.

"This is all wrong," Kalyn said, digging through the suitcase.

"Let's go," he said, pushing her out of the way and shutting the suitcase. "We don't have time for this."

"All right. Just let me change." It was going to be a very long vacation.

CHAPTER TWENTY-SIX

Sterling waited impatiently at Logan International Airport. He hadn't seen Laila since he had left California and her flight was due to land any minute. His brother sat beside him, looking bored and ready to leave. Alistair spent the whole break talking about Rebecca. Sterling knew his brother was anxious to get back and find her.

Sterling saw her. Her strawberry blonde hair bounced jauntily and her violet eyes peered through the crowd. Sterling waved, not caring that he looked like an idiot. From the corner of his eye, he saw his brother stand up.

"Is she finally here? Can we go now?"

"Yes, we'll go to baggage claim and then we'll leave." Sterling watched Laila fight her way through the crowd, running straight for him. He opened his arms to give her a big hug and just as she got close, Alistair stepped in front of him. Laila laughed in surprise but couldn't stop. She ran straight into

Alistair and squealed as he picked her up and spun her around.

"Did you miss me?" he asked as he set her down.

"Maybe a little," she said, a bright smile on her face.

"Yeah, that's what I thought," Alistair smirked and finally let her go.

Laila danced out of Alistair's arms and into Sterling's. He didn't waste any time and took her face in his hands, kissing her like he hadn't seen her in years.

"Okay, you two, that's enough. Can we please leave?"

Sterling moaned and rolled his eyes. "Yes, we can leave now." Tennille wasn't coming back to school until Sunday which meant he had two nights alone with Laila.

The three retrieved Laila's bags and Alistair led the way to the car. They reached the parking lot and Alistair started to slow down. Sterling pulled out his keys and unlocked a huge, black SUV.

"What happened to your Mercedes?" Laila asked curiously.

The brothers looked at each other. "Alistair totaled it. Mom and Dad made him pay the down payment on this one."

Alistair rolled his eyes. "I still don't believe that it was totaled. You just wanted a new car."

"Either way," Sterling looked back to Laila, "he wrecked my Mercedes."

"Where's your Lexus?" Laila asked Alistair who threw her bags into the spacious bed of the car.

"In the shop. I'm picking it up next week."

"If you'd bought an automatic, like I told you, you wouldn't keep burning the clutch," Sterling reprimanded his brother.

"I can drive a stick! It's just a shitty car!" Alistair said defensively as he climbed into the back seat.

"So, what's up with the three ton environmental wrecking ball?" Laila teased.

"Oh, but look," Sterling said, pointing to a little green symbol on the side of the tank. "It's a hybrid. Looks like your crazy California hippie ways are rubbing off on me."

"Hmm, it's about time."

CHAPTER TWENTY-SEVEN

"Laila! You're back early!"

Laila turned around to see a rosy cheeked Rebecca down the hallway. She dropped her bags, walked to her friend, and gave her a big hug.

"I didn't get to see you on the last day of school." Rebecca paused and glanced at Sterling. "How are you?"

"Great," Laila answered, "And you?"

"Amazing," Rebecca answered. "I've got so much to tell you!"

"Yeah? About what?" Laila led the way back to her room.

"About Randy," she finally whispered.

Sterling walked in and dropped the luggage. "Laila, I'm going to put my bags in my room and park the car. I'll be back in ten minutes." He made sure to emphasize the time.

"Okay." She knew he was eager to get her alone.

"Ten minutes," he mouthed behind Rebecca's back and Laila nodded, shooing him away with her hand. She closed the door.

"Okay, tell me everything!" Both girls sat down on the bed and smiled at each other.

"You first," Rebecca insisted. "What happened the night of the party?" Laila hadn't had a chance to tell Rebecca about everything that had happened with the prescription. She had spent every minute with Sterling after they reconciled and then a few days later everyone left for vacation.

Laila tensed a little at the thought of that party but felt that she could trust Rebecca. It felt good to connect with another girl.

"After you left with Randy, Chase and I were dancing when Sterling found us and completely flipped out. He accused me of cheating on him with Chase and showed me a prescription for Plan B with my name on it."

Rebecca nodded.

"Someone had forged it and left it for everyone to find. When Sterling found out about it, he freaked out. It didn't help that Alistair repeated a rumor that Chase and I were sleeping together every Thursday after our tutoring session."

Rebecca winced. "Do you think he freaked because of what happened with Kalyn?"

Laila nodded. "I didn't even know that they had been together. But he explained everything to me the next day and long story short, everything is fine. It's great, actually."

Rebecca smiled. "I'm really glad you two worked things out. You really are one of those couples that just make sense, you know?"

Laila laughed. "Kind of. Now you! Tell me everything!"

"Okay, get ready, because you aren't going to believe this." Rebecca sat up straight. "So, last night Randy came back early from break and we decided we should probably catch up on all the studying we didn't do. We were going to go to the library but decided his room would be more convenient"

"Let me guess. You didn't study."

"No, not at all," Rebecca dismissed Laila's comment as if it were outrageously obvious. "We were messing around, things were getting a little heavy, and then he asked me to be his girlfriend."

"Well, that's great!"

"It was so sweet and he was so nervous but that's really not the best part," Rebecca laughed in anticipation of her story.

"Okay, let's hear it," Laila said, very intrigued.

"So one thing led to another and we ended up, you know," Rebecca paused to let Laila figure out what she meant.

Laila giggled. "How was it?"

"Short."

"Short? You mean his little Randy?" Laila raised her pinky finger slowly and Rebecca burst into laughter.

"No, not that. The sex. It didn't last very long. I'm thinking maybe 45 seconds."

"What happened?" Laila tried not to laugh but Rebecca clearly found it amusing so she didn't feel as bad.

"He was a virgin," Rebecca whispered.

"You didn't know that?"

"How was I supposed to know? We never talked about it. He didn't say 'Wait, before I stick this in, you should probably know that this is my first time.' He didn't say anything!"

Laila rolled on the bed laughing. Rebecca did the perfect impression of Randy.

"How did you know?"

"I didn't," Laila told her. "I just thought you would."

"Well, I didn't either. And then, totally awkward, he made this comment about how he had expected it to last longer and I asked if it usually did and that's when he said he had nothing to compare it to."

"I can't believe he didn't tell you!"

"I know!"

"So what did you do?"

"I got angry with him. I mean, I unknowingly took his virginity. That's a huge deal."

Laila nodded her head in agreement.

"But we talked about it," Rebecca's face calmed and her eyes started to twinkle. "He said he had been waiting for the right girl."

Laila gushed. "That's really sweet."

"And then he made it up to me."

"Oh, I don't know if I want to know how," Laila teased.

Rebecca laughed and raised her fingers to her lips, making an obscene gesture with her tongue which threw both of the girls into an uncontrollable fit of squeals and giggles.

"I don't know how he got so good at that," Rebecca said once she was able to regain control. "But it was like, I don't know, I couldn't even believe it was happening." She laughed again when she didn't know what to say. "Three times! It happened for me three times, Laila, in one go!"

Laila's side was hurting from all the laughing but she couldn't stop. "Oh my God!"

"I know! And since then, he's all I've been able to think about."

"I bet!"

Rebecca looked at her. "Thank you."

"For what?"

"I think, if I hadn't met you, I would never have allowed myself to fall for Randy. You've been a really great friend."

"Rebecca," Laila smiled and leaned over to hug her. "That's really sweet."

"I mean it," Rebecca said, hugging Laila close. "Thank you."

"Well, you're welcome." Laila really didn't know what else to say. Rebecca's honesty touched her.

"I should get going. Randy's waiting for me to meet him for dinner," Rebecca winked.

"Meet you for lunch on Monday?"

"Yes," Rebecca said without hesitation. "I'll see you at 12:30?"

"I'll be there."

"Bye." The brunette closed the door just in time to see Sterling running down the hallway, his eyes turning from anxious worry to relief when he saw Rebecca leaving the room.

CHAPTER TWENTY-EIGHT

𝕽ebecca had just finished her makeup when she heard knocking on her door. Slightly annoyed because she wasn't dressed yet she swung her legs off the mattress and stood up. "One second," she called to whoever was on the other side.

She found her bathrobe and wrapped it around her nearly naked body. She loved it when her roommate wasn't here—she could walk around in nothing but her underwear. She opened the door to see Alistair Pierce standing in the hallway. He looked like a complete mess but still unbelievably handsome. His hair stood out at all angles, his cheeks were red, and he wore rumpled clothes. It looked like he had just rolled in from the cold.

"Hi," he said softly. "Can I come in?"

"No," Rebecca said. "I mean, I don't think that's a good idea."

"Please? I just want to talk."

"Talk?" She spoke slowly. This was a new one for him. "You've never wanted to just talk."

"I know. But there's just something I have to tell you. I wanted to run over her the minute I got back but my parents called."

Rebecca sighed, contemplating her options. She didn't want to let Alistair into her room or into her life. She had found happiness without him and having him barge in unexpectedly was already taking its toll on her nerves. She wanted nothing more than to find her razor and cut until the anxiety melted away. But she knew he wouldn't stop bothering her until she let him have his say.

"Fine," she said.

He walked in and sat casually on her bed.

"Rebecca, I don't want you to be angry with me."

"Why would I be angry with you?" She folded her arms across her chest.

"Because of how badly I've used you..."

"No, Alistair," she cut him off. "I knew what I was doing every time I slept with you. I was angry with myself because I kept pretending that one day you would actually want me. I knew that day would never come but I was too far gone to let myself see it."

"I've been horrible to you for years."

"But then," Rebecca interrupted him again, "I grew up. I met someone who actually cares about me. Someone who isn't afraid of making a commitment."

"But you can't actually like him! It's Randy!"

Rebecca laughed. "Of course I like him. He's good to me. He takes care of me."

"I could take care of you."

"No, you couldn't. Or you won't."

"But I will," Alistair said quickly, taking a step towards her and reaching for her arm. "Rebecca, I've missed you so much. Not seeing you every day, not being able to touch you, it's been hell for me. I need you and if you would just give me another chance, I'm ready to commit, I'm ready to do whatever it takes to keep you happy."

"To keep me happy? Alistair, you can promise these things but nothing about the past three years would make me believe you could keep that promise."

"Look," she said, gently touching his arm. "I'm not upset. You don't want a girlfriend and that's fine. I shouldn't have tried to force you into it so many times. But I want to be in a relationship, that's just who I am. So please just accept the fact that Randy and I are together. You might even be happy for me."

"Are you happy?" He asked quickly.

"Yes." He took her wrist in his hand, slowly turning it up toward the ceiling. He pushed back her bathrobe and looked at her arm. No fresh cuts. He dropped her arm and picked up the other one but found no cuts.

She pulled her arms away and crossed them again. "I think you should leave."

Alistair shook his head. "No. Show me your legs."

"No!" Rebecca stepped away from him, shocked he would even ask.

"If I knew that you were truly happy with him, then I would leave. But I won't believe you until I've seen that you aren't hurting yourself."

"I'm not showing you anything."

"Please?" Alistair pleaded with her and closed the space between them. His hands were on her hips, holding her still as she looked away from him. Tears welled up in her eyes. Slowly, he bent to his knees, pushed her robe apart and gasped. Her inner thighs were smooth and soft, not a scratch or burn on them.

"Stomach," he commanded, pulling at the sash of her robe.

"You aren't going to find anything, Alistair. I haven't cut myself in weeks."

He pulled her robe open and stared at her exposed stomach. Nothing. His eyes roamed her body as her robe fell to the floor.

"Is this what you wanted?" she sobbed, tears falling from her eyes as she stood perfectly still. "To get me naked, humiliate me?"

"No," Alistair said quickly, reaching down and picking up her robe. He put it around her shoulders and covered her naked body. She felt him move in close and place a gentle kiss on her lips.

"I came here tonight because I wanted to tell you how sorry I am," he said, his face remaining close to hers. "I came here tonight to tell you that I love you and that, if you'll forgive me, nothing would make me happier than to spend the rest of my life making sure you are never hurt again."

She had waited so long to hear him say that and now that he had, she wished he had kept his mouth shut.

"Why now, Alistair?" she asked, closing her eyes for a long second and smelling his sweet breath as he stood so dangerously close. "I've loved you for three years and you wait until I've moved on to tell me this."

"Have you really moved on?" he asked. "I think you still love me." His hand stroked her neck and she could feel herself starting to lean into his touch. No, she was done with Alistair, she was stronger than this. Randy didn't need to use these seduction techniques. As a couple, they were above all the games and the drama.

"Of course I do." She hung her head and took a step back, still not completely out of his reach. "But I'm with someone else now. Someone who doesn't take three years to make up his mind. Someone who has shown me that he can make me happy."

"But he's not me," Alistair said with confidence. "You know that as happy as you may seem right now, you could be much more so with me."

"I'm sorry. But I won't break his heart."

"Fine. I'm going to try and wait for you but I probably won't last long. You and I both know you're making a mistake. But if you can move on, then so can I."

Rebecca looked up at him. Was he really going to move on? If he did, that might make it easier for her to forget this conversation ever took place. "I've known for years that we belong together. That's why it's so hard to tell you goodbye."

"So don't do it."

"I have to," Rebecca said with conviction. "It's a new reality now and I belong with someone else. You have to leave. I want you to go."

He paused just before he left and stood at the threshold. Just leave, she said to herself, before I change my mind.

"I love you," he said before closing the door behind him.

CHAPTER TWENTY-NINE

"Julian, what are you doing here?" Tasha opened the heavy front door to her house. She shuddered at the blast of frigid Vermont air. He looked good with a slick haircut and slightly tanned skin from the French sun.

"I called earlier today and your dad told me you were catching the train back a day early. I came to offer my chauffeuring services."

"Are you also going back a day early?"

"If you'll allow me to take you, I most certainly am."

"Where's Kalyn?" Tasha asked. She hadn't invited him in out of the cold.

"Spending one last evening with her parents," Julian answered quickly. "She didn't see the point in returning early."

"And if you leave with me today, how will she get to school tomorrow?" She knew that Kalyn would have a driver.

Julian shrugged. "Does it matter?"

Tasha laughed. "Not really."

"So, you'll come with me?"

"Why not? My bags are in the foyer. I'll be right back."

"Wait," Julian stopped her and pushed himself into the doorway. "I'll get those for you."

Tasha stepped aside and stared at Julian as he scooped up her luggage. His behavior was peculiar, to say the least. She said goodbye to her parents and followed Julian to his car, curious to see where this would go.

He held the door for her and she climbed in, amused at his chivalry. Julian only looked at a girl when he wanted to sleep with her. Certainly, he must know that it wasn't going to happen. She didn't sleep around like most of the other girls at school and she had no intention of becoming one of Julian's sluts.

"So," she started when Julian climbed in the car. "Why are you really here?"

Julian laughed. "You are blunt, aren't you?"

"I've just never seen the point of flitting around the truth."

"But you're usually so perceptive. You should be able to tell me why I'm here."

"If I knew, then I may never have allowed you to drive me back to school."

Julian laughed again. "You probably shouldn't have allowed it. But you're here now."

Tasha turned in her seat to look at him and waited for an explanation. Julian just stared at the road.

"So tell me!" She finally laughed.

"I came today with every intention of telling you how I feel about you."

"And how do you feel about me?" Tasha blushed. This was a surprise.

"I like you, Tasha. But my parents are pushing for a summer engagement and a winter wedding. I'm supposed to marry Kalyn in less than twelve months."

That soon, Tasha thought. Poor guy.

"Knowing that I have to spend the rest of my life with someone I despise or lose my inheritance and the favor of my parents, makes me want to spend as much time as I can with you. Because, even though I've been with a few girls, you're the only one I've actually wanted to talk to. You're the only one that I really want to be with right now."

They drove in silence for a few minutes.

"A few girls?" Tasha's finally said. "Has it really only been a few?"

"A handful, at most."

"At most?" Tasha asked.

"What do you want me to say? I'm not proud of the number of girls I've slept with. I'm not proud that I've broken hearts, Kalyn's repeatedly. But I thought that I needed to sleep with as many girls as I could before I was bound to one that I didn't love. I thought I needed to get it out of my system, so to speak. And now that I've lived that life, all I want to do is to find someone who challenges me, someone I could spend a day with and not tire of, someone who won't give in to my every request."

"And you suppose that I would want to spend a day with you, challenge you and refuse your every request?"

"Wouldn't you?" Julian grinned at her.

"It wouldn't be a total waste of my time."

"So then, today it is. We'll spend the entire day together, just you and me."

"What do you expect out of today, Julian?" Tasha asked quickly.

"I expect nothing from today." He shifted in his seat.

"You're lying."

"I'm not," Julian insisted. "I would be lying if I said I wasn't hoping for something out of today, but I'm not expecting anything."

"What are you hoping for then?"

"I'm hoping that you'll find me…" he paused for a moment searching for the right words. "Intriguing and honest. Just as I find you captivating and beautiful."

Tasha didn't know what to say. Speechless. It had been ages since she had been at a loss for words. Captivating and beautiful?

Tasha had never fallen for anyone. Most guys at Harper's were incredibly immature or acted with a single-track mind. Sex. That's all they wanted. Julian had always been completely off limits but that didn't mean she hadn't found herself daydreaming about him. He was by far the best looking guy at school and, when he wasn't being a jerk and trying to sleep with some freshman or sophomore, he could be quite interesting. He liked to travel and enjoyed discussing philosophy, music, and art. The two of them had enjoyed many deep conversations while Kalyn sat impatiently beside them, complaining about being bored.

"So," she said, changing the subject. "Have you decided what school you're going to next year?"

"Not yet," Julian replied. "You?"

"Columbia," Tasha said with a smile.

"Columbia? Are you and Kalyn going to be roommates?"

"She didn't tell you?"

"Tell me what?" he asked

"Kalyn didn't get in to Columbia. She wasn't even waitlisted."

"Well, that's too bad. I know she was hoping to get in there."

"You know she'll go wherever you go, right?"

"Has she even applied to NYU?" he asked back.

Tasha shrugged. "Probably, but who knows?"

"Tasha," Julian said quietly, "what happened to her?"

Tasha took a deep breath. She knew Julian and Kalyn used to be close family friends. The three of them often spent summer days together at Kalyn's pool when they were younger. Kalyn had always lacked tact and rarely used common sense, but she had once been bubbly and kind.

"I wish I knew. It wasn't like it came out of nowhere, but the change happened so suddenly."

"I blame our parents," Julian said quickly.

Tasha nodded, understanding he wanted some kind of justification for Kalyn's behavior. "Her behavior is a direct reaction to your situation, no question about it. But there is something inside of her that made her react the way she did. Don't get me wrong, no one would react well to that kind of helplessness and pressure, but she's taken it too far. She's not in control of her future so she's doing anything she can to control and manipulate her present."

"Have you always been so smart?"

Tasha laughed. "Yes. But that's only a theory and I'm done talking about Kalyn."

"I think I agree with you," Julian said, shifting into fifth gear. As he moved into the left hand lane, his hand settled on hers. For a moment she almost pulled away out of habit. But fighting the impulse, she kept her hand still, wondering if he was playing a game or if he had truly thrown in his towel.

CHAPTER THIRTY

February passed slowly for Alistair. Rebecca seemed to be everywhere and he knew she felt like hell inside. He could tell by the forced smile she flashed when he saw her with Randy. He could tell by the way she stared blankly in class and snuck glances at him when she thought he was looking away. He hoped that she would change her mind and give him another chance, well actually a fiftieth chance.

Friday night arrived and Alistair looked forward to getting drunk and forgetting the whole thing. Impossible. He tried but he kept seeing her face.

He brought a bottle of bourbon to Tasha's, hoping she would be willing to share a drink and listen. He had prattled on to Sterling and Laila for an hour before they had gotten bored and kicked him out. Laila had been sympathetic, of course, saying it was very brave of him to even try. But as Rebecca's friend, she wasn't much help. Sterling hadn't been as nice. He laughed at Alistair, not hesitating to say he'd told him so.

Tasha would be able to give him real advice. Tasha would be encouraging. He knocked on the door and waited impatiently for her to answer it. When it finally opened, he wanted to kick himself.

"Hey, Alistair!" Kalyn smiled at him and he narrowed his eyes.

"Hi, Kalyn. Is Tasha here?"

"Ugh," Kalyn groaned. "No, she's gone again. I've barely seen her at all this semester. I have no idea where she goes."

"Do you know when she'll be back?"

"No idea. Is there something I can help you with?"

"No, I'd really rather speak with Tasha," Alistair said, turning away.

"Alistair, wait," she called after him. "If this is about Rebecca, then I think I might have some good insight for you."

Alistair stopped and slowly turned his head. "Kalyn, no offense, but I don't think you are the best person to get advice from."

"Okay, so it's not really advice. I just think we could help each other."

"What do you mean?"

Kalyn stepped aside and pushed the door open. "Come in. We can talk."

Alistair looked down the hall hesitantly. He knew he shouldn't trust Kalyn with anything—certainly not his feelings for Rebecca—but if she had an idea of how to help him, he would listen. The two of them had been friends once.

190

"How can you help me, then?"

"Well," she began, "as you can probably see, Julian has all but lost interest in me. He's been screwing around with the entire sophomore class and embarrassing me in the process."

"So? What does that have to do with me?" Alistair could really care less about Kalyn and her problems.

"Julian generally doesn't care who I sleep with or go out with. I think the only person who could make him jealous would be your brother."

Alistair rolled his eyes and interrupted her. "I'm not going to convince Sterling to hook up with you."

"I'm not asking you to do that. I've given up hope that he will ever love me again. But you and your brother look so much alike. Julian may think that I'm clinging to some part of Sterling if we were to get caught in a compromising position."

"If what? Do you really think that if we sleep together and Julian finds out, he will assume you're just going for the next best thing? No offense to your fiancé, but he doesn't seem like the type to really put two and two together."

"Just a date, that's all I'm asking for."

"A date? You want me to take you out on a date?"

"You wouldn't have to pay for anything. Just pick me up in front of the dorms and drop me off a few hours later. We can go out for pizza or McDonald's or something."

"As much fun as that sounds, Kalyn, what good is it going to do me?" He tried to understand her twisted mind and felt a headache coming on.

"Well, you want Rebecca back, don't you? I mean, that is why you're here, isn't it, to get Tasha's advice on how to do it?"

"Yes, I want her back," Alistair said mournfully.

"Then just think about it. When was Rebecca always the most attracted to you? When was she always begging for you to take her back to your room?"

It seemed so long ago since he had been with Rebecca and he hated to remember her begging and pleading. He had been horrible. Alistair shook his head and shrugged his shoulders.

"Wasn't it always after you had slept with someone else?"

"I don't know."

"Remember what happened after you slept with Kelly Horowitz last year?" He wanted to forget Kelly. "Rebecca was so determined to win you back that she dragged me to the mall so I could help her pick out new lingerie."

"Oh, yeah." Alistair smiled at that memory. Rebecca had looked amazing that night. She had come to his room wearing an oversized rain coat which she stripped off and dropped to the floor. Beneath it, she wore something black, lacy, and sheer. At the time, he hadn't realized that Rebecca had worn it out of desperation. What a fool he had been.

"I don't know, Kalyn. It seems like a lot of trouble to go through just in the off chance it actually works."

"Why wouldn't it work? If Rebecca thought you had really moved on, then I guarantee you she would come crawling back."

"I don't know." Alistair stood up and looked around. It seemed like a good plan, kind of. And Kalyn did have a point; Rebecca always seemed to pay more attention to him, seemed to want him more, after he had been with another girl. It had worked in the past, so why wouldn't it work now?

"Just think about it," Kalyn suggested, walking to the door and opening it for him.

"If I did agree, and I'm not saying I'm going to, when would we do this?"

"Next Thursday," Kalyn said as if he should have known.

It seemed like an odd day but Alistair didn't think twice about it as he walked out of the room and down the hall, still clutching his unopened bottle of bourbon.

 ## CHAPTER THIRTY-ONE

Tasha stared at Julian out of the corner of her eye. He yawned and then returned to watching the screen. She could see he was bored with the plot, and so was she, but a theatre was the safest place for them to rendezvous. The room was nearly empty except for a middle-aged couple near the middle row and a few younger kids in the front.

She saw him sigh and turn his head toward her. He leaned in ever so slowly but she had to stop him when his lips drew too close.

"Julian, stop." She smiled and turned to him. The pouty look on his face made her giggle. Giggle? Tasha had never giggled but something about Julian brought that out of her.

"I can't help it," he whispered, his hand reaching for hers on the arm rest. "We've been on eleven dates and you haven't let me kiss you yet. I'm getting desperate."

"Eleven? You've been counting?"

"Oh, I've been counting," he said with a sly smile. "We've been out eleven times and I'm beginning to think you don't like me at all."

"Don't you dare play those games with me, Julian Polk. You know they won't work."

"What is it then? Why won't you kiss me?"

His dark brown eyes looked black in the dim light. He searched her face for an answer. She knew he cared about her. Just the fact that he had stayed celibate for a month said a lot. Still, none of that removed the main impediment to their relationship.

"You're engaged. And even though I know you don't love her, it won't hurt any less when you leave me for her."

"So if you keep your distance physically, you can also keep your feelings away emotionally?" One dark eyebrow rose as he asked the question.

"I'm so close to the edge, Julian. You have no idea how close. If I let you kiss me, I won't be able to hang on. I won't be able to forget about you once you've left me."

"I've tried to get out of it, Tasha," Julian explained, getting frustrated. "What more do you want me to do? I brought it up again with my parents when I was in France. My mother, maybe she can be convinced. But my father wouldn't even listen. What can I do?"

"Nothing. I'm not asking you to do anything. I'm just explaining why I can't do anything, either."

"Can't or won't?" Julian scoffed as he sat back in his seat and turned back to the screen.

"Both," Tasha said sharply as she continued to look at him. "We wouldn't be doing ourselves any favors by taking this any further than it's already gone."

"What are you saying?" Julian turned to her.

"I'm not saying anything," she sighed.

"Are you breaking up with me?"

Tasha laughed. "We aren't even together. How can I break up with you?"

"But you don't want to see me anymore?"

"I didn't say that," she said softly. "I'm just saying that we aren't making things easy on ourselves. And I'm saying that I won't allow myself to do anything more than hold your hand. That way, I don't have to worry about falling for you. That's my kryptonite, got it?"

"I knew it! You are falling for me!" he screamed. The couple in the middle row turned and glared at them. "Tasha, what if I told you that I would end things with Kalyn? What if I did it tonight?"

"You need to think about this," she warned him. "Think about everything you are going to have to do without. How are you going to pay for college? You would be throwing away a lot on the chance that this will work."

"A chance to love you," he reminded her. "A chance to be happy for once in my life. A chance that you might learn to love me back. I'll take that chance."

"Julian, this decision can't be made spontaneously just because you have a crush on me."

"No, that decision isn't spontaneous. I've been thinking about it for weeks, months now. This decision, however, could and should be made spontaneously."

Julian's hand cupped her cheek, reached around the back of her neck and pulled her to him. Their lips touched and Tasha's world turned upside-down. Julian kissed her gently and she kissed him back. She wanted to protest but her heart won the battle against her head.

Julian kissed her long and deep, teasing her tongue with his just for a moment before he pulled away. "See, that wasn't so bad."

Tasha opened her eyes and sighed. "Not so bad. I hope it's all you can think about when you breakup with Kalyn and confront your parents."

"A kiss like that is motivation enough to get me through just about anything."

PART II-

End

Game

CHAPTER THIRTY-TWO

Thursday, 6:05 PM

Rebecca sat in the library with Randy. The library was safer. In her room, they would eventually get naked and he would see what she had done. She had made it so long without Alistair but it had finally caught up to her. Even Randy's love hadn't been enough. She didn't want him to see the cuts.

Randy had agreed on the library. He always wanted to make her happy. But since the night Alistair confessed his feelings, she hadn't been able to stop thinking of him. Her mind spun in circles. He had made her miserable for three years and she tried to tell herself that he couldn't be trusted. As much as she tried to convince herself that he was lying, he was only trying to fool her to get her back into bed, her heart wasn't listening.

So she had escaped into the shower that afternoon, brought out her razor, and cut her leg. The blood had seeped from the wound, cooling her nerves. She relaxed between passes with the razor. She hadn't meant to take it as far as she did, but it was like visiting an old friend, an old friend who was an incredibly bad influence. When she finished, her right leg looked like a bloody stump. She liked the look of the red blood splattered against the black and white tiles, and waited a while before cleaning it up.

Now she sat in the library with Randy, his head hung low over their text book. She looked away, searching the stacks for something distracting to look at. She still cared for Randy, enough that she felt incredibly guilty for not being able to give him her complete devotion. She sighed deeply, knowing that things were going to have to end soon between them.

"Are you all right?" She heard him ask.

"I'm fine."

"You haven't been acting fine."

"I've been worried about college stuff."

"You've been thinking about Alistair, haven't you?"

Shit, Rebecca swore to herself. Was it that obvious? "No. Why would you say that?"

"I see the way you look at him in the hallways, in the cafeteria, in class."

"I get it," Rebecca snapped, knowing she had been caught.

"It's pretty obvious you still have feelings for him." Randy sighed. "I guess I shouldn't be surprised."

"What's that supposed to mean?" Rebecca asked, reaching for his hand.

"I've known that you've never gotten over him. I guess I was just hoping that you would learn to love me as much as you love him. Then maybe one day you could learn to forget about him."

Tears welled up in her eyes. "Why did you even bother with me at all? If you knew you could get hurt, why would you even bother?"

"It was a chance I was willing to take. I'm not scared of getting hurt, Rebecca. I've been picking myself up and moving on my entire life," he said, looking deep into her brown eyes. "I just wanted to be with you. Even for a few moments, a few days, however long I could get. I wanted to say that I'd had the chance to touch you and care for you. To dream and pretend that you really cared for me in return."

"Randy," Rebecca's voice cracked as she spoke, tears streaming down her face. "You have made me happier than anyone has ever made me. And I do care about you. I care about you so much."

"But it's not enough?"

"I wish it were," she sobbed quietly, burying her face in his neck. "You are everything that I need and everything that I want in a guy. I wish I could help how I felt about him because he really doesn't even compare to you."

"Then why?" Randy pushed her away so he could look at her. "Why can't you just forget about him?"

"I want to, so badly. But I just can't. I'm so sorry."

Randy shook his head. "I hope you find happiness, Rebecca. You deserve to be happy."

"What will you do?" she asked.

"What does anyone in my situation do? I'll learn to move on."

She sobbed and hung her head, ashamed to let him look at her. She'd broken his heart, something she never wanted to do.

"Hey," he said softly, lifting her chin. "It's better that it happened now. We could have let this go on for far too long."

"Randy, thank you for showing me what things should be like."

Randy smiled and leaned in to kiss her. He pressed his lips against hers just for a second before pulling away and standing up. "Goodbye, Rebecca."

"Goodbye," she choked out before turning away and burying her head in her arms. His footsteps echoed across the floor and faded away. After a few minutes, she sat up and collected her books and highlighters. Where was Laila? Normally, she would be tutoring Chase but he had showed up at 5:00, waited twenty minutes and then left. It was so unlike her to blow off tutoring and Rebecca needed her now. Oh, well, she thought. She would go to her room.

Still numb, she walked into the cool February night. The snow had melted but the crisp smell of winter and the scent of burning wood hung in the air. She had done the right thing letting Randy go. She could have never made him as happy as he deserved to be while still hung up on Alistair. He deserved so much more.

She hadn't seen Alistair with another girl since he had professed his love. She wondered how he would react when she told him about Randy; when she told him she was his once again, forever and always.

Her smile faded as she approached the building. Sterling's huge, black beast of a truck idled outside the front door. Dim light reflected off the driver's side window and inside, she saw Sterling's silhouette, his blonde head leaning toward someone in the passenger seat, kissing her. Had Laila ditched Chase's tutoring to go on a date with Sterling? As Rebecca walked parallel to the car, Sterling pulled away and she saw Kalyn's face.

Rebecca gasped. It couldn't be. Sterling would never cheat on Laila – especially with Kalyn. Yet she had seen him in the car with his ex-girlfriend's hands roving all over his body. She couldn't bear to look at it.

Laila would be crushed, humiliated and heartbroken. As much as she didn't want to be the one to tell her, someone would do it sooner or later. At least Laila would be able to cry on her shoulder.

Rebecca ran past the car, forgetting everything she was going to tell Alistair, and darted up the stairs to Laila's door. She knocked furiously until it opened. Laila stood in a tank top and pajama shorts, a huge smile on her beaming face.

"Hi Rebecca, what's up?"

"It's Sterling," Rebecca said slowly. "I just saw him in his car with Kalyn."

Rebecca watched Laila's face sink into confusion. She felt heartbroken at having to deliver the news.

CHAPTER THIRTY-THREE

Thursday, 3:29 PM

*K*alyn walked quickly to Chase's room. With Alistair in, she needed Chase's help to put the rest of the plan into action. She reached his room and let herself in.

"Can I help you with something?" Chase asked, surprised to see her.

"There is something I need to talk to you about."

"Can you knock next time? What do you want?"

"I need you to disconnect the battery of Alistair's car."

"What?"

"Disconnect the battery of Alistair's Lexus," Kalyn repeated.

"Why would I do that?"

"Because I need you to do it." Did she have to explain everything to this dolt?

"I don't see how…"

"You don't need to know. Just do as I say and I'll make sure that Laila is in your arms by the end of next week." He was so dumb, so predictable, and so easy to manipulate.

"I don't know. This seems like an awful amount of trouble to go through."

"Chase," she reprimanded him and put her hands on her hips. "Don't tell me you've given up on her. Don't tell me you don't want her anymore."

"I didn't say that," Chase snapped back. "I like Laila but this seems awfully..."

"Chase, spare me your ramblings. If you want her to remain with Sterling, just tell me to leave." He considered her words for a moment. What went on in that thick head of his?

"I'll do it," he finally replied. "But if this plan of yours doesn't work, then I'm out."

"This will work. Trust me."

"Kalyn, you are probably the last person I would ever trust."

"Just make sure to walk Laila by the front of the dorms at exactly 6:30. I'll do the rest."

CHAPTER THIRTY-FOUR

Chase waited a few minutes before following her out the door. Did he really want to do this? He didn't want to hurt Laila. She had turned out to be one of the few genuine people in this place.

He thought of her smile, her hair, her breasts and legs, and continued walking, knowing he only had a shot if she broke up with Sterling. Kalyn, on the other hand, was pure evil. But sometimes, and hopefully in this case, evil could be harnessed for good.

He had never disconnected a car battery before but assumed it would be easy. He strolled casually to the parking lot, passing the Volvos and BMWs before coming to Alistair's silver Lexus. Getting under the hood without being able to pop the button from the inside would be difficult but he'd seen someone do it on a cop show and knew he could figure it out.

Chase circled the car once, looking for an open door, before putting his hands on the hood and running his fingers around the crease. He could feel the latch and he tugged. Nothing happened. Glancing around to make sure no one was watching, he pulled an Amex Black card out of his wallet. He pushed the latch back with the thick plastic and heard the hood snap open. Success!

The next part proved trickier. He had never really seen inside the hood of a car. Donald, their handyman, usually took the car for an oil and grease job or for repairs. The engine looked as foreign to Chase as Greek in a textbook and he looked around, frustrated, unsure of how to proceed. Didn't people die trying to jumpstart cars? Could he electrocute himself by pulling the wrong wire? He felt his confidence melting away.

Chase reached for something that looked like a car battery. He spotted a few wires and prepared to give one a strong pull when his phone vibrated in his pocket.

"Shit," He reached deep into his jeans. He started to open it, still keeping his eyes on the battery in case it tried to jump up and run away from him, but the phone slipped through his fingers, bounced off the bumper and shattered as it hit the cement.

"Fuck!" He bent down to pick up the remnants of his phone. But it was pointless. The phone wouldn't turn on. He cursed again and he reached into the belly of the car and started yanking violently at any wire he could reach. If Alistair knew anything, he would certainly be able to see that someone had purposefully sabotaged his vehicle. But that didn't matter to Chase. No one was around and if he could get back to the dorms without anyone seeing his grimy hands, he would be in the clear.

He slammed the hood of the Lexus before running back to his room. The clock read 4:33 and he looked forward to seeing Laila at 5:00 in the library. The thought of her voice and soft laughter calmed him. He could replace his phone tomorrow. He would fuck Kalyn one last time this weekend and then, if all went well, Laila would become the girl in his life. Girlfriend? He had never had one of those before and the idea sounded like something he could get used to.

CHAPTER THIRTY-FIVE

Thursday, 4:30 PM

Kalyn waited impatiently for Alistair to pick her up. If Chase screwed up, she'd kill him. Standing outside the dormitories, she tapped her foot and craned her neck toward the parking lot driveway. A slow smile spread across her face as Sterling's black SUV pulled onto the road in front of her. It was such a ridiculous car, or rather, truck.

She knew Alistair wasn't looking forward to their "date", and frankly, neither was she. She kind of liked Alistair, Sterling's alter-ego, but he had been in such a foul mood lately that she barely recognized him anymore. He pulled the car in front of her and then ran around the hood to open her door. More than a few people watched, curious looks on their faces. From this distance, she knew none of the other students would be able to tell which Pierce twin she was with.

Good, she thought to herself. The more people who saw, the faster the rumors would spread. And

Alistair's solemn face made him look even more like his brother. She hopped inside and shut the door, the low rumble of the engine calming her nerves.

"So, where are we going?" she asked when her date climbed into the driver's seat.

"Pizza," Alistair said quickly. He hadn't bothered to put on anything nice. He wore grungy jeans and a dirty jacket. His hair was a greasy, tousled mess. What a wreck.

They drove in silence, ate in silence, and lingered in the restaurant, in silence. Finally, after three sodas, Alistair paid the bill and stood up, gesturing for Kalyn to follow him. But it was barely 5:45 and she needed to keep him distracted for another forty five minutes.

"We should get some ice cream," she suggested.

Alistair grimaced. "If you want."

"You aren't having fun?" She laughed at his mood.

"I'm just..." he spoke slowly and then paused. "I'm beginning to think this wasn't the best idea."

"Maybe not. But it certainly won't hurt anyone, now will it?"

"I hope not."

"Just a little while longer, enough to get people really talking, and then we can go back," she promised him.

Alistair sighed and turned his attention to the football game playing on the flat-screen behind Kalyn's head.

"Where's the Lexus?" Kalyn asked innocently when they finally got back in the car and started to drive.

"It wouldn't start," Alistair sighed. "Piece of shit has been giving me trouble for months now."

"I thought you just got it last year."

"I did," he offered nothing more.

"Hmmm. My mom says that for graduation she's letting me pick out a new car. Any suggestions?"

"Nope."

Kalyn sighed. "Alistair, look, I know you aren't happy right now. But you can at least try to be nice for the next hour or so. It will make this a lot easier."

"No, what will make this easier is if we keep our mouths shut. I'm feeling incredibly deceitful and rotten right now and I'm trying not to blame you. I know I agreed to do this but unless you want me to start screaming at you, you'd be wise not to say another word."

Kalyn looked out the window and took a deep breath. She really didn't care that Alistair didn't like her. She didn't really expect him to after what she had done to Sterling but all of that would soon change. Alistair would forgive her and see that Laila was just a passing fancy to Sterling. In time, her ex-boyfriend would come to appreciate her again as well. Of course, eventually the fantasy would end. She would have to marry Julian and then it would be the two Pierce twins against her once more. But that didn't matter. She would savor her time with Sterling. It would make the rest of her miserable life easier to bear.

She kept silent and let him drive in his sullen anger. She couldn't have timed the drive back any better. Her watch read 6:30 and Chase would soon be walking Laila back to her dorm. She dug her nails into the palm of her hand, pinching the sensitive skin between her thumb and pointer finger. Her eyes started to water from the pain and she looked out the window, sniffling lightly. Alistair didn't say anything to her but she knew she had him. Foolish boy.

"Kalyn, what's wrong?" he asked, clearly annoyed but too much of a gentleman to let a girl leave his car crying.

"Nothing," she squeaked out. "It's just, never mind."

Alistair sighed. Boys never liked to see a girl cry. It drove them crazy.

"You can tell me," he pushed. "Look, I'm sorry. I shouldn't have said what I did, but this whole thing with Rebecca, it's got me so crazy. "

"Thank you," she whimpered, finally turning to face him.

His face looked soft and so much like his brother's. Kalyn blinked slowly and was able to imagine, just for a second, that it was Sterling staring back at her with his blue and green eyes. She glanced toward the library and when she didn't see Chase and Laila walking toward them, she knew she would have to stall a little longer.

She reached for Alistair's hand on the center console. "I'm sorry I dragged you into this. It really was a stupid idea."

Alistair shook his head. "It's all right. I'm sorry I was such a shitty date."

Kalyn smiled up at him, her eyes softening. She could see someone moving toward them. "You look so much like him," she said quietly.

Alistair looked sympathetic. "Kalyn, you shouldn't compare us."

"I know. But I can't help it. I miss him so much."

"Don't do this to yourself."

Kalyn nodded and reached for his face. If she had done her job right, he would accept her approach. He would try to comfort her. Don't move back, she mentally willed.

Their lips touched for a long, lingering moment. Her fingers combed through the short hairs at the back of his head and then she finally pulled away.

"Thank you," she said sweetly before glancing around. "I feel much better. I should probably go."

Alistair nodded and smiled at her. "Things will get better, you know."

"I know." She flashed him a brilliant smile. Boys, men, they were all so easy to play.

CHAPTER THIRTY-SIX

Thursday, 3:41 PM

"**B**ut just look at the envelope!" Laila cried. "It's so small!"

"Laila, mine was small, too." Sterling said. She paced the floor of her room, alternating between handing Sterling the letter from Yale and opening it herself.

"But my acceptance letter from Stanford was huge," she replied.

"Every school is different. Now open it."

"I can't." She sat down on the bed next to him. "This is everything. This is you and me and if I didn't get in then it will really suck."

"If you didn't get in, all it takes is a phone call," he reminded her.

"But if they didn't accept me the first time then maybe I'm just not supposed to go to Yale."

"Then we'll go somewhere else."

"Stanford is the only other school I would consider and I wouldn't dare ask you to go with me."

"Why not?" He reached for her hand and brought it to his lips.

"Because you would be miserable there. You belong at Yale."

"And so do you," he smiled at her. "But most of all, we belong together. Now open this so you can stop worrying."

Laila took a deep breath. She had been waiting for the letter since Monday when Sterling had received his and had been obsessively checking her mailbox ever since. But when it finally arrived, she had been unable to open it. She took the letter from Sterling's hand and closed her eyes, imagining what it would say, willing it to be true. She ripped through the envelope and quickly unfolded the paper inside.

"I got in," she whispered.

Sterling kissed the top of her head and then her lips. It felt like only her skin held her body together and pure bliss threatened to explode from her every limb.

"There's so much to do before we go!" Laila said, pulling away from him and standing up.

"There's nothing we need to do this very second," Sterling laughed.

"I know but I don't think I can sit still right now." She started pacing again. "Because pretty soon we'll be registering for classes and buying our books, meeting our new roommates."

"Wow, slow down. We haven't even graduated from high school yet. We have to do that and then there's a whole summer." He reached for her hand

and she immediately felt herself calming down. "And you already know your roommate," he added with a smile.

"I do?" She looked confused.

"Don't you want to live with me next year?"

Laila blushed, walked over to the bed and stood between his legs. "My parents would kill me," she said, running her fingers through his styled blonde hair.

Sterling reached up and put his hands around her waist. "Mine would be thrilled."

Laila looked down at his face. Her hands brushed his hair from his forehead. She could imagine what it would be like coming home to Sterling every evening after classes. He would wait for her at the door and she would throw herself into his arms, allowing him to carry her to the couch or bedroom where they could make love for hours. Before it had been a day dream. Now it seemed closer to reality.

"Sterling?" She asked softly as his hands started to travel down her hips.

"Yes?" He looked up at her and a tear almost came to her eye. He was so handsome, so perfect for her in nearly every way.

"Will you make love to me?"

Sterling's hands froze on the back of her thighs just below the curve of her bottom. His eyes went wide and his mouth dropped. "What, like right now?"

Laila smiled and had to swallow a laugh in her throat. She nodded slowly and her hands left his hair to unbutton her skirt.

She watched Sterling's face as he carefully studied each of her movements. His eyes blinked rapidly as she unwrapped the navy skirt from her hips and let it fall to the floor. She held her breath as he reached for the inside of her thigh, his hand lightly wrapping around and moving up and down her leg.

Laila hadn't planned on today being *the* day. Luckily, she had chosen to wear a cute pair of underwear. Her heart raced and her hands shook as she reached for Sterling's shirt. She fumbled with the first few buttons and giggled when Sterling became impatient and finished the job for her. He stood up and rolled his shirt from his shoulders.

"Laila," he said huskily, drawing her to him and kissing her deeply. She waited for him to pull away and say something else but he didn't. With their lips still locked together, he picked her up and wrapped her bare legs around his waist. Laila grabbed his strong shoulders and kissed him deeply, with the pent up hunger of months of waiting. He moved quickly to the door and she squeezed her thighs around him. His hand left her leg to lock the door. He turned off the lights, kissed her again, and then laid her on the bed.

"Laila," he whispered again, reaching for her face in the darkened room. "I love you so much. I want you to know, before anything happens, that this moment means the world to me. You're giving me something that I know you value and cherish. So just know that I'm going to cherish it as well. This will be something that we share together."

A tear rolled down her cheek. He bent down and kissed her lips before kissing away the tear. She wrapped her arms around his neck and pulled him closer. They kissed until her body relaxed and felt ready.

The physical act of making love was better than she had expected. Sure, it hurt, and it was quite a messy business when she really thought about it, but it was also exciting and thrilling to feel him so close and to know that she was taking such a big step in their relationship and also in her life. Sterling had been careful and had taken his time, whispering to her how amazing she felt and constantly checking to see if she was in too much pain.

"That was awesome," Sterling said after a moment of silence. He sounded totally content. "I don't even know how to describe it, and it was only our first time. Just absolutely amazing."

His head rested next to hers on the pillow, his breath tickling her neck. She smiled at his inability to put his thoughts into a complete sentence and heard him sigh.

"What are you smiling at?" he asked.

"Nothing," she turned her head to look at his face.

"Liar," he accused. "Was it my performance?"

Laila laughed and pushed herself closer. "Your performance was perfect. Everything was perfect."

"It was, wasn't it?" Sterling mused, closing his eyes as Laila kissed his chest. "Are you hurting?"

"Not much," she told him honestly, kissing his neck.

221

"Do you need anything?"

"Nothing," she said breathily. "Just hold me."

"Are you sure you're okay?"

"Everything is perfect," she assured him again. "You're here and I'm kind of numb, but I feel great."

He held her close and had almost drifted off to sleep when he heard her soft voice.

"Sterling? Will you hand me my phone?"

"Of course," he said, kissing her head and reaching behind him to the nightstand.

He watched as she flipped it open and started texting someone. She closed it quickly and handed it back to him.

"What was that about?" He asked.

She smiled and nuzzled against his chest again. "Just letting Chase know that I won't be making it to the library tonight. I don't think I ever want to leave this bed." Her arms wrapped around his waist. He kissed the top of her head and pulled the comforter around her shoulders. If she had her way, they would never leave this room. They would remain in bed and in each other's arms for all eternity.

CHAPTER THIRTY-SEVEN

Thursday, 6:33 PM

Rebecca knocked furiously at the door until Laila opened it. Finally.

"Rebecca, what's wrong?"

"It's Sterling," Rebecca said slowly. "I just saw him in his car with Kalyn."

Laila looked confused and Rebecca felt terrible for her. Laila shook her head and looked back into the room.

"Sterling's been here all afternoon," Laila finally replied.

"No, Laila, I just saw him," Rebecca said sympathetically. Oh, poor Laila, she was in denial. Rebecca knew about being in denial and she also knew that honesty would help her friend more than anything. Laila needed to hear the complete truth. "He was in his car and Kalyn's hands were all over him."

"Rebecca, he hasn't left this room since classes ended." Sterling came to the door wearing only khaki uniform pants. He looked so much like Alistair that Rebecca did a double take. Then it hit her.

"Oh, God," she said softly. Alistair had been in the car with Kalyn. The thought of them together made her stomach turn. "I have to go."

Laila looked concerned. "Rebecca? Are you all right?"

"I'm fine. I'm sorry. I just have to go," she paused and looked at the couple standing in the doorway. Sterling's hand lay protectively on Laila's shoulder, his bare chest leaning just slightly into her back. It was so obvious that he loved her, so clear that he would never hurt her. She should have known all along that Sterling would never have been in the car. She took a deep breath. "You two are perfect, you know that?" She managed to smile a bit. "I'm sorry I bothered you, I really am. Laila, I'm really glad you're happy with him. You deserve someone as great at Sterling."

It had been Alistair. It had been Alistair, her Alistair, in the car with Kalyn, a girl she used to call her closest friend.

"I have to go," she said again, turning from the door and leaving the couple standing bewildered.

"Rebecca?" She heard Laila call to her. But she didn't turn around. She couldn't turn around.

Sterling whispered something and after a few seconds the door closed. Swallowing her sobs, Rebecca walked quickly to her room. She ignored her roommate and pulled out a piece of paper from her notebook. Scribbling a quick note, she wiped the tears

224

from her eyes, folded it and wrote a name before placing it on the desk.

Grabbing her towel and shower caddy, she practically floated to the showers, her head dizzy. It felt like walking through a cloud. An eerie numbness filled her body and the only thing she could feel were the shoes on her feet, the tears on her cheeks, and the towel in her hand.

"Rebecca? Where are you going?" A familiar voice brought her head out of the clouds.

"Julian, hi," she stammered, not recognizing her own voice.

"Are you all right?" Julian asked. "You look really pale."

"I'm fine," Rebecca lied and smiled. "But you can tell your fiancée that she's a backstabbing whore."

"Do you want to talk about something?"

"No. I'm fine." She smiled and continued floating.

"Rebecca, wait," Julian said, reaching for her arm as she walked by.

The touch of his hand shocked her and she stopped dead in her tracks, feeling as if she had run into a brick wall.

"Julian," she said, her voice sounding irritated and disappointed. "Please let go of me."

"I will," he hesitated and didn't let her go. "Just please come with me. I'm on my way to Tasha's room and I would really like it if you came with me. I don't think you should be alone right now," he said quietly and she pulled her arm away from his hand.

"What makes you say that?"

"I don't know, you just look really upset."

"What makes you care all of a sudden? I mean, why do people do that? Why do they pretend to care or suddenly realize that they care only once it's too late? Once you've moved on, once you've made up your mind to move on? Don't they realize they are messing with people's lives?"

Julian shook his head. "Whatever happened, I'm sure that it won't seem as bad tomorrow."

She smiled, not because what he had said made her feel better, but because she knew that he was completely wrong. "I guess you're right," she said, trying to appease him.

"So you'll come with me?"

Rebecca shook her head and lifted her shampoo slightly. "I'm going to shower first. I'll meet you there in a few minutes."

Slowly, he nodded and Rebecca took a few steps away from him before he hung his head and went on his way. Rebecca reached the showers and undressed quickly, hanging her robe on the inside of the shower door. She couldn't feel the warm water. Rebecca looked down at the yellow shower caddy. The bright sunflowers seeming so juvenile, so mocking.

She picked up her old friend. The pink plastic safety casing broke away easily enough. Safety, security, happiness – it was all just an illusion. "Pick your poison," she said to herself as she looked down at her already mutilated leg. But her arms were smooth and inviting. She pushed the razor deep into her skin, looking away as the blood started flowing. She felt a nauseous wave in her stomach and she inhaled deeply, forcing it to subside. Closing her eyes, she made another pass, pushing as deep as she could. Then made another and another.

Rebecca opened her eyes, staring at the red stream running down the drain. Finally she felt something again. But even that started to numb with the warm blood that flowed from her wrist. She smiled. Free. Free from Alistair and Kalyn and Harper's. Her knees gave way and she relaxed on the tiled floor, her back against the shower wall, the water cascading over her head, her arm hanging limply by her side. Blood continued to seep into the shower. She closed her eyes and thought of Alistair. He had loved her. He had loved her and that was enough to make her happy, even if it no longer mattered.

CHAPTER THIRTY-EIGHT

Thursday, 6:55 PM

Alistair threw the dorm door open and strode into the hallway. He felt like shit. Guilt and remorse filled him and he knew the only way he would feel better was to confess to Rebecca and beg her forgiveness.

"Hey, Alistair," he heard Laila calling to him and he saw her standing outside her room looking confused.

"Hi, Laila. Have you seen Rebecca? I need to talk to her."

"I'm just going to look for her. Have you seen her today?"

"No, why?"

Laila shook her head, looking more distraught. "She came to my room a little while ago saying something about Sterling and Kalyn together in his car. She wasn't making much sense."

"When? When did you see her?" Alistair ran to Laila and grabbed her arms. Rebecca had seen them together.

"I don't know, maybe twenty minutes ago."

"Shit!" He swore and took off running in the direction of Rebecca's room.

"Alistair? What happened?"

But he didn't answer her. He burst through her door and winced as Rebecca's roommate jumped in surprise.

"What is going on?" Hailey asked.

"Where is she?" Alistair yelled, looking around the room.

"She took her shower stuff and left," Hailey answered, looking annoyed.

Laila walked into the room.

"Where is she?"

"Shower," Hailey and Alistair answered in unison.

"Okay. You stay here, and I'll go look for her."

"I'm going with you." He glared at her. She had never seen him this upset.

"Alistair, you can't. Just wait here."

He sat down at Rebecca's desk, ignoring Hailey's glares. She clearly wanted him out. He closed his eyes and rubbed his temples. If Rebecca had seen him with Kalyn in the car just now, it would ruin any chance he had left. How could he have been so stupid? He hung his head and looked down at Rebecca's desk, a piece of paper with his name on it

229

catching his eye. Slowly he reached for it, straightening the letter in his hands.

Alistair,
It was always you. I will never stop loving you.
R

The handwriting looked sloppy and rushed. With shaking hands, he slammed the paper down on the desk and ran towards the girl's showers. Before he could get there, he heard a piercing scream. He threw the door open and nearly slid on the slick tiles. Alistair turned the corner, following Laila's cries. Laila stood propped against the tiled wall, her breaths ragged and her entire body quivering as she stared at the floor in front of her. He skidded to a stop in front of the open shower door. Rebecca lay slumped against the tiles, her face pale, eyes closed, curly brown hair hanging around her naked shoulders. Water rained down on her still body. Blood trickled from her wrist and pooled around her leg and hip. A gentle smile turned her pale lips.

Alistair reached for her hand and even though her skin still felt warm, he knew there was no life left in her. "Rebecca?" he whispered. "Rebecca? Baby, wake up." His voice cracked as he fought against a sob. "Rebecca, wake up!" Alistair dropped her hand and cringed as it fell to the floor with a splash. Laila whimpered and gently touched his arm. She looked so scared that it shocked Alistair back to reality. Clothes soaked, face wet with tears, he slowly turned from

Rebecca and reached for Laila, pulling her into his chest to muffle her crying. She fell into him limply, resting her entire weight against him. He turned around so that she wasn't facing her dead friend, holding her as tight as he could. His back hit the wall and he prayed that when he opened his eyes she would no longer be there. But she was. The girl he loved lay dead in her own blood, and it was his fault.

Mechanically, his hand reached into his pocket and he retrieved his cell phone. He numbly dialed 9-1-1 and waited for it to ring.

CHAPTER THIRTY-NINE

Thursday, 7:06 PM

Kalyn skipped down the hallway to her room. She wanted to celebrate. Certainly Tasha would have something to drink and might, if she asked nicely enough, choose to celebrate with her. She found her roommate sitting on her bed, smiling to herself as she read a book.

Tasha looked up as Kalyn came bursting through the door. "What are you so happy about?" Tasha asked, looking back at her book.

"I'm happy because I'm a genius."

"Really? What did you do to earn genius status?"

"I have, with only minimal effort, broken up Laila and Sterling."

"And how did you manage to do that?" Tasha put her book down

"I kissed her boyfriend."

"You kissed Sterling?"

"Not exactly," Kalyn laughed to herself. "I was with his twin brother, in Sterling's car."

232

Tasha shook her head in disbelief. "What makes you think she would fall for that?"

"What makes you think she wouldn't?"

Tasha laughed. "She's not an idiot, that's what."

Kalyn opened her mouth to protest but the door flung open and slammed against the wall. Chase stood there looking distraught. Kalyn smiled at him but he frowned.

"I couldn't find Laila," he said quickly.

"What?"

"She didn't show up at the library and wasn't in Sterling's room."

"Did you check her room? Did you think to call her?" Kalyn's mood dropped like an anvil. Had she just wasted the entire evening with Alistair for nothing? She didn't relish making an ass of herself.

"My phone broke when I was … when I dropped it earlier."

"Okay, it's okay," Kalyn said. "Someone saw us together and with any luck they'll think it was me and Sterling. Rumors are bound to get around and everything will be fine."

"You and Sterling? What are you talking about?"

"Shut up, Chase!" Kalyn screamed and started pacing back and forth.

Tasha picked up her book and her sweatshirt and moved toward the door. "I'm outta here," she said. Chase stepped aside to let her out and Julian filled his space.

"Have you two seen Rebecca tonight?" Julian asked.

"No," Kalyn answered, dismissing him with a flick of her hand.

Tasha shook her head.

"Well, I think someone should go find her. I just saw her heading to the showers and she didn't look so good."

"What was wrong with her?" Tasha asked looking worried.

"I couldn't get much out of her. She wasn't making much sense."

"Why should I care about Rebecca?" Kalyn asked, glaring at Julian.

"Because she's our friend," Tasha replied.

"She hasn't been our friend for months," Kalyn reminded her.

"When I passed her in the hallway, she asked me to tell my fiancée that she is a backstabbing whore," Julian said slowly.

Kalyn gasped and pushed past Chase, stepping towards Julian. "Wait! Did she say why?" Her mind spun. Even though Chase had nearly ruined her entire plan, if Rebecca saw them together then word was bound to get around.

"What did you do, Kalyn?" Julian looked at her coldly.

"Nothing. I did nothing," Kalyn lied.

"Kalyn, you just said you were with Alistair." A scream cut off Tasha's next sentence. Tasha pushed past Julian and Kalyn, taking off toward the shower room. Julian and Chase quickly followed her and

Kalyn jogged reluctantly behind as the screaming continued.

Kalyn rounded the corner and heard the screams coming from the bathroom. Tasha slowly pushed the door open and she followed them in. Laila whimpered in Alistair's arms. Rebecca lay under the shower water, pale and naked, surrounded by blood.

Tasha gasped and instantly turned around burying her face in her hands as Julian's arms surrounded her in a protective embrace.

"Chase, go call an ambulance," Julian said as he held Tasha securely to his chest.

"No, no! Rebecca!" Kalyn couldn't believe the sight. She stepped closer and shook her head to dispel the image. This must be a dream, a terrible nightmare. Chase ran out of the bathroom. She looked for a friendly face, someone to console her, but they had all turned away. Alistair sat on the floor with a crumpled Laila in his arms. Tears streamed down his cheeks and he held the blond close. Tasha shook in Julian's arms and he glared at her.

"What did you do?" her fiancé asked her.

"I did nothing," she said, shaking her head.

No one spoke. Broken sobs echoed off the tiles, mixing with the steady hiss of running water.

"She saw us, Kalyn." Alistair's voice said mournfully from the floor.

"No, she couldn't have. What was she doing there?"

"She did," he snapped at her.

Kalyn shook her head violently. This wasn't her fault. This couldn't have been her fault. "I didn't think anything like this would happen."

"We didn't think at all!" Alistair screamed causing Laila to cry harder. "We did this!"

Kalyn shook her head. Hateful. They were all hateful. It wasn't Kalyn's fault Rebecca was so troubled. The poor girl. Anyone could have seen that she was weak, barely able to make it through a normal day without mutilating herself. Everyone knew Rebecca wasn't strong enough, didn't they?

Kalyn started backing away from the showers. The door opened and campus security rushed into the room.

CHAPTER FORTY

Friday, 3:26 AM

"Laila, please just close your eyes and try to sleep," Sterling pleaded.

"I can't," she whispered back. "Whenever I close my eyes, I see her. Should I have known?" Laila asked.

"No. You couldn't have known."

"But you should have seen her legs. They were covered in cuts and her arms had scars all over them. How did I not see what was happening? I could have stopped her." Her voice trailed off.

Alistair had never mentioned Rebecca cutting herself but Sterling had heard rumors about it. Girls would see or hear her in the bathroom stalls but no one tried to reach out and help. Kalyn wasn't capable of doing that and Laila couldn't stop punishing herself for not noticing.

Sterling didn't know what to say to assuage her guilt. So he pulled her close on the bed, rubbed her back, and kissed her head.

"You should try to sleep." But he knew it would be a sleepless night for both of them.

* * *

Alistair looked at the clock in his room. It was almost 3:30 in the morning and he had been lying in bed for nearly two hours. He couldn't believe that she was gone. He had watched the medics zip her into a body bag and wheel her out of the building on a stretcher. He still held the note gently in his hand, the paper still perfect. He didn't want to mar her last words.

He was glad Sterling had Laila. She needed someone right now. She blamed herself but he was the real villain. He put his arms behind his head and looked up at the ceiling. He would always love her.

* * *

Chase hurled the empty bottle against the brick wall of the library and watched it shatter. Things had gone so terribly wrong and he hated himself for letting Kalyn use him. He hated himself for not searching for Laila when he should have. Perhaps if he had, Rebecca would be alive.

He crunched through the icy grass, the campus spinning. Vomit rose in his throat and he fell to his knees before heaving onto the lawn. But the second he closed his eyes, he saw Rebecca's lifeless face and her pale, naked body lying sprawled on the shower floor.

He pushed himself off the ground, stepping in his own vomit as he ran. He didn't know where he was running. He just knew he had to get away.

* * *

Julian and Tasha lay in his bed. They hadn't spoken in over an hour. Tasha felt Julian turn toward her and she relaxed onto her side so she could look at him.

"I'm calling my parents tomorrow morning. I don't care if they disown me, refuse me my inheritance. I can't marry her."

Tasha reached for his face. She knew after what had just happened he had no other choice. She had always known, but tonight confirmed it. "Are you going to tell them what happened?"

"I think they should know," Julian said. "I don't really care about the money but they deserve to know why I'm making this decision. It's not an act of rebellion."

Tasha smiled. "Well said."

Julian kissed her lightly on the lips. "Will you still love me when I'm broke and on scholarship at Columbia?"

"Yes."

"Will you marry me? By tomorrow I will be single again." One dark eyebrow playfully rose.

"No."

"Okay. I'll ask again next year."

* * *

Kalyn snored lightly. A bottle of sleeping pills lay open on her nightstand. She had planned on taking one every thirty minutes until she fell asleep. It had only taken three. She moaned and turned over, pulling her sweat-soaked sheets up to her chin.

***

Randy cried onto his damp pillow. He had been walking back from the cafeteria when he heard news of an incident. Someone had died and the police and campus security were questioning several students. Curious, he had walked down the hallway. Hailey stood outside a crowd of students. She looked horrified and even sadder when he approached.

"I'm so sorry," she had told him. It took him a moment before he understood why she said that to him. He only cared about Rebecca and Tennille at Harper's, and Tennille was in New York with Tate. Rebecca.

Laila ran out of the bathroom and into Sterling's arms. Tears streaked her red face and her eyes looked puffy and swollen. He gleaned a few words from the police: suicide, razor, blood, and felt a deep sadness. The police tried to clear them away but he stayed glued to the spot. Eventually a stretcher bearing a black body bag emerged from the bathroom. Kalyn walked past everyone, in a trance. Julian and Tasha held hands and hung their heads. What had happened to her?

Alistair emerged last and Randy ducked behind an officer to keep from running into him. Alistair's face drooped so low it could scrape the ground. He had never seen anyone look so guilty. Randy instantly knew who to blame. He waited a few minutes before returning to his room, his head spinning with confusion and anger.

He lay awake, staring at the crack in the ceiling, wondering if there was anything he could have done. Was he too hard on her in the library? Should he have held on longer in the hopes of saving her? He didn't know. He didn't even know why she took her own life. But he would find out and make that person pay.

CHAPTER FORTY-ONE

"**M**om? Can you please ask Dad to pick up the phone? I need to speak with both of you."

Tasha sat by Julian's side and clasped his hand. The phone receiver clicked.

"Hello, Julian. What's the problem?"

"Mom, Dad, there's something I have to tell you." He paused and took a deep breath. "I'm not going to marry Kalyn."

Silence.

He continued, "Last night, something terrible happened and I wanted to tell you about it before you heard it from the dean or from the Andrettis. Kalyn's friend, Rebecca Valencourt, killed herself."

His mother gasped and his father cleared his throat.

"She slit her wrist in the girls' bathroom. Her best friend found her. We ran to help but we were too late."

"Julian, what does this have to do with your engagement to Kalyn?" his father asked and his mother sighed.

"Blake, let him finish," she said quietly.

"No, it's okay," Julian said. "Before Kalyn and I were forced into this arrangement, she had been in love with this guy, Sterling Pierce. She broke up with him to be with me and to honor her parents' wishes, but she never really let go of the feelings she had for him. This year, Sterling started dating someone new and Kalyn didn't take it too well. Last night she did something really extreme."

"What are you talking about?"

"She somehow convinced Sterling's twin brother Alistair to take her on a date. She wanted to make Sterling's girlfriend jealous but Rebecca saw them and thought that Alistair was dating Kalyn."

"Julian, stop all of this nonsense."

"Dad, will you just let me finish?" He squeezed Tasha's hand a little tighter. "Rebecca had been in love with Alistair for years and when she saw him kissing Kalyn in the car, she snapped. Kalyn had been one of her best friends and Alistair had been playing with her heart since freshman year. The sight of them together was, I guess, more than she could take. She went straight to her room, grabbed a razor and killed herself. The cops said she had probably only been dead a few minutes before we found her."

Julian listened to the silence nervously until his father spoke. "If what you are saying is true, then it is just as much this Alistair boy's fault as it is Kalyn's."

"I'm not blaming anyone, Dad. Rebecca had problems and clearly needed help. All I'm saying is that I can't marry someone who could betray her friends like that. I'm not marrying someone who would go to such lengths to win the heart of a boy she has no future with. I will not marry Kalyn."

More silence and Julian held back the tears.

"If you like, I'll call the Andrettis myself. I won't tell them what I've told you but I'll break the engagement and they won't blame you. You can save your friendship and the company."

"We'll talk to them, sweetie," said his mom.

Julian waited for his father to say something. "Dad?"

"Son," his father said in a broken voice. "I'm sorry about your friend, Rebecca. And I'm sorry that Kalyn has shown such dishonorable behavior. I respect your feelings on this matter but I think you should consider what you are doing by breaking this engagement. You have a lot to lose."

"I know what I'm doing by breaking this engagement," Julian interrupted his father. "I'm choosing to live my own life; I'm finding my own happiness. I don't love you or respect you because of my trust fund. I love you because you are my parents, because you raised me and encouraged me to think for myself. And that is exactly what I'm doing."

"If you respected us, you would consider who else will be impacted by this decision."

"And if you loved me, you would only want what's best for me."

In the long silence that followed, Julian realized how tightly he had been gripping Tasha's hand. Finally his father spoke. "Is your mind completely made up, son?"

"It is," Julian replied with confidently.

"Then, for the time being I have nothing else to say on the matter."

Julian closed his eyes in frustration. He had known it wouldn't be an easy conversation, and he had known the possible ramifications, but a definite answer from his father would have given him an idea of how the future would play out. He hated ambiguity but at least he was now free.

"We'll discuss this further on Sunday when you come home for dinner," his father added.

"Will the Andrettis be there?"

"No," his father added quickly. "This will be strictly a family dinner."

Julian blinked his eyes and took a deep breath. "Thank you."

"Do you need anything?" his mother asked, relief in her voice as well.

"No, I'll be all right. I'll see you on Sunday."

"We love you, sweetheart."

"I love you, too, Mom."

Julian heard the phone hit the receiver and he waited to see if his father would say goodbye. He could still hear him breathing on the other end. But he didn't say anything and Julian ended the call.

Tasha wrapped her arms around his neck and he held her close.

"How do you feel?" she asked.

"Like shit," Julian said with a laugh. "But incredibly liberated."

"Are you going to talk to Kalyn?"

Julian sighed. "Not today." Kalyn had left early that morning for her parents' house. He needed to speak with her face to face.

"Do you want to get out of here? Spend the day in town?" Classes had been cancelled and all of the students had been milling about, gossiping and asking questions.

"That sounds like a great idea," Julian said, taking her by the hand and helping her off the bed. They grabbed their jackets and walked quickly down the hall, ignoring the curious stares of their classmates.

CHAPTER FORTY-TWO

One week. It had been exactly one week since Kalyn had walked into the girl's washroom and seen Rebecca Valencourt lying dead on the floor. She hadn't quite come to terms with it. Sometimes she still expected to see Rebecca wandering the halls, sitting in the cafeteria, studying with Randy in the library. But she was gone. Kalyn had watched as they zipped her body into a bag and wheeled her from the bathroom.

Classes had been cancelled that Friday, and all students who felt they needed extra time to grieve had been excused from classes throughout the following week. Kalyn had gone home for a few days but didn't find much solace there. Her parents were away and the big, silent house felt more like a morgue than a home. After two days, she had returned to Harper's, for better or for worse, to face her demons.

She slept and cried, then pulled herself together long enough to walk to the cafeteria only to receive glares from the other students. The hostility only caused more crying and more pill popping. She had nearly depleted the stash she had stolen from her mother's medicine cabinet. Desperate for more, she had gone to the nurse, who said no, and then to Tasha who also refused to help her. Typical bitches.

She knew, ultimately, she just had to get through it. She had to find someone to talk to, someone who understood her and would listen. Since Tasha wasn't willing to help, Julian wouldn't speak to her, and her parents would only refer her to a therapist, Kalyn sought out the only person she had left: Alistair. He had been through all of this with her and probably felt the same guilt.

She walked quickly to his room, keeping her head down to avoid the stares. She knocked quickly and waited for the door to open. Sterling's solemn face greeted her, eyes sad, shoulders hunched. Kalyn's eyes prickled with tears when she saw him. He had been her reason for all of this. Her foolish and selfish greed, her boredom and pride had made her do something terrible. Looking at him now, she remembered why she loved him, she remembered why she left him, but she couldn't remember why she had hurt him.

"Kalyn, I don't think you should be here," Sterling said. His voice sounded soft and tired.

"Is Alistair in there? I really need to see him." She barely recognized her own voice. It had been almost two days since she had spoken to another human being.

"I don't think he wants to see you," he said rather apologetically.

"I know he doesn't, but I have no one else." Kalyn hung her head and blinked back the tears.

"Al?" She heard Sterling say. No one responded and she waited for him to slam the door in her face. But he didn't. Sterling stepped aside and Kalyn looked up. Alistair sat on his bed, his head against Laila's shoulder as she held him, whispering something into his ear. Neither looked at Kalyn as she stepped into the room. Laila continued to whisper and Alistair's head nodded in slight understanding. Soon, Laila's hands lifted his face and she kissed him on the forehead.

Alistair looked at Laila as if she was the Virgin Mary. Hadn't Laila been Rebecca's best friend? Hadn't she encouraged her to date Randy and to forget about Alistair? Why would she be comforting him now, after everything he had done? Why was it that Alistair had people who cared about him, who would hold him and kiss his forehead, when Kalyn had no one?

Kalyn stared longingly at the two people on the bed, wishing she had someone to comfort her and tell her everything was going to be all right. Laila slowly stood up from the bed and walked to Sterling.

The shorter blonde looked straight past Kalyn as she stepped aside to let the couple pass. Laila knew what she and Alistair had done. Sterling must have known as well. She didn't understand why they didn't rip her to shreds. Why had they even allowed her into the room?

"What do you want, Kalyn?" Alistair said before the couple had even left the room. But she waited until the door closed to speak.

"I just want to talk."

"There's nothing to talk about," he said, staring at the blue sheets of his bed.

"Alistair, please? I need to know that what we did isn't the cause of all this."

"Of course it was the cause! What we did? We killed someone, Kalyn. That's what we did."

"No," she said quietly, shaking her head and crying. "She killed herself."

"Because of what she saw us doing!" Alistair screamed at her suddenly. She could see him shaking with rage. "Fuck! How the hell did you talk me into that? Was it worth it for you? Did you get something out of it?"

"No. I would do anything to take back that night."

"So would I! But we can't! We fucking can't and now she's dead!"

Kalyn sobbed and stumbled to his bed, wanting him to calm down and reason with her. "Alistair, listen to me," she said, looking deep into his blue eyes. "We were trying to do something right."

"No! There wasn't anything right about it. You were playing some sick, twisted game. You couldn't have cared less if Rebecca took me back. So tell me, what were you really in it for?"

Kalyn shook her head and Alistair rolled his eyes. "I was trying to win your brother back."

"Excuse me?" Alistair's brow rose in shock.

"Chase and I had this plan. He was supposed to walk Laila by the car on the way back from the library so she could see us together and think you were Sterling."

"You could have just talked to me about it. I would have told you, without any of this fucking bullshit deception, that he would never love you again."

Kalyn closed her eyes and sobbed. She knew he was right. "I know and I'm sorry. God, Alistair, I'm so sorry."

"I'm sorry too. I'm sorry my brother ever looked at you. I'm sorry I was desperate enough to play your stupid, fucked up game, I'm sorry…" he started to say something else but paused when he heard someone knocking at the door. "Go the fuck away!"

Alistair jumped off the bed and stormed towards the door. Talking to him had been a mistake. Kalyn had only angered him and made herself feel worse in the process.

"I want you to leave. Don't try to talk to me again. I'm not your friend. I'm not a shoulder to cry on. You'll find no sympathy from me," Alistair said and glared at her. They both jumped at another set of knocks. "What?" Alistair screamed.

He reached for the knob but before he could get there, the door flew open.

Randy stood in the doorway, his face stern and his eyes glassy.

"Randy, now is not a good time." Alistair glared at the redhead.

"I wanted to find you alone," Randy spoke very deliberately and slowly. "I'm sorry she has to see this."

He reached into the pocket of his jacket and pulled out a hand gun. He extended his arm and pointed it at Alistair's head.

"What the hell, man? Put that away!" Alistair started backing up and tripped over his own feet, stooping to catch his balance.

Kalyn inched her way toward the wall, making herself as small as possible.

"How could you do it?" Randy looked straight at Alistair. "She was beautiful and she loved you. All she wanted was for you to love her back. But you were too preoccupied with yourself to appreciate her and notice her pain." His voice started to quiver and the hand holding the gun began to shake.

"Look," Alistair said calmly, "I know you cared for her. But so did I."

"Bull shit!"

"I loved her," Alistair pleaded. "I loved her more than anything. I know I fucked up. I know that we can never have her back and I'm sorry that I took her from you, from all of us."

"Took her from me?" Randy interrupted. "She had already left me when she saw what you did!"

Alistair looked doubly pained, if that was possible. "Put the gun down, Randy. Killing me isn't going to bring her back."

"Bring her back?" Randy raised his free hand and wiped away the tears from his eyes. "I know nothing can bring her back but she deserves retribution!"

"If you could feel the pain inside of me right now, you would know that she will never be forgotten, never be replaced. Let me live with the pain. Let me live with the knowledge that I lost the one thing I cared about because of my own stupidity."

Randy's entire body started shaking. "I hate you," the redhead whispered before he closed his eyes and pulled the trigger.

CHAPTER FORTY-THREE

Chase heard the roar of a gunshot. He stopped dead in his tracks and craned his neck toward the sound. A second blast shook the hallway. He took a few tentative steps in the direction of the shots, waiting to see if the shooter would emerge into the hallway. No one came and he picked up the pace.

He reached the door to Alistair and Sterling Pierce's room. The smell of gunpowder laced the air and Chase peered inside. Randy lay on the floor, a dark puddle near his head.

Alistair sat slumped against his bed, his eyes closed, his face pale. Just above him lay a blonde girl, her body sprawled across the comforter. Chase didn't know what to do. He felt frozen in place. Looking back at Randy, Chase took a small, tentative step forward. He maneuvered around the redhead and moved toward the bed. Beautiful blonde hair, designer clothes — the girl was Kalyn.

Blood splattered the wall behind her and soaked the pillow where she had fallen. Her face was nearly unrecognizable, the gaping wound stretching from her eye to her ear. "Oh my God," Chase whispered as he took another step forward.

"Is she dead?" Alistair whispered from the floor. "He was aiming for me."

But Chase couldn't answer. He knew she was dead but he didn't want to say it. Footsteps and voices came from outside the room. Slowly, he reached for her. He had shared so many secrets with Kalyn, shared so many moments. Their relationship had never been love, more like a mutual understanding, but the site of her dead still shook him. She had become bitter but he still remembered her smile, her warm body, and her beautiful eyes.

Someone pulled at his arm. Perhaps they would let him touch her skin just one last time, feel her soft hair as it glided through his fingers. Hands pushed him onto the floor beside Alistair. Students gathered around them, some crying, some screaming, but Chase only saw Kalyn's dead body, the perfect face gone forever. He tried to remember the last thing he said to her but his mind wouldn't focus and his tears wouldn't stop.

CHAPTER FORTY-FOUR

"Sterling! Stop teasing me!" Laila laughed.

Sterling's strong arms hugged her tightly. "I'm not teasing you. I just don't think I'm in the mood anymore."

"Then get off!" Laila laughed again, pushing against his chest in a pointless effort. He didn't budge. "My parents could be here any minute!"

Slowly, Sterling lowered his hips and watched Laila close her eyes and smile in pleasure.

"I thought you weren't in the mood," she said.

"I'm always in the mood when I'm with you," he replied before he bent his head to kiss her.

Laila passionately kissed him back, his full lips soft and warm. Each time they made love, Laila swore it was better than the last. Sterling was so strong and powerful, yet so gentle with her and so attentive. Nothing escaped his attention.

Laila kept her eyes open so she could watch his face, appreciating his every expression. She enjoyed the intimacy of making love more than the physical delight: the knowledge that Sterling was so deeply in love with her, the comfort of knowing she had saved herself for someone she loved with all her heart, and the satisfaction of giving Sterling such complete pleasure. She knew he would always take care of her first and she smiled as he recognized the look of restraint on her face. She wanted them to finish together, just like she preferred.

He smiled back at her in understanding, adjusting his pace. Laila closed her eyes and whispered his name, their bodies shuddering together. Sterling collapsed on top of her. His weight on her body felt comforting and she knew she could be content to stay like this forever. "I love you," he breathed into her ear as he held her close.

Laila smiled and opened her eyes, running her hands across Sterling's naked shoulders and back. He had put on even more muscle since the beginning of the year, spending hours in the gym with his brother. Alistair used the burn of lifting to erase the pain of his guilt. Alistair had changed so much since "the event," as the rest of the school referred to the tragedy.

Laila wouldn't have recognized him if she hadn't been spending so much time with the twins. For months, Alistair hadn't smiled, his dimples gone into hiding. And for months he only spoke to Sterling and Laila, having become completely dependent on them for company and solace. Laila didn't mind. She knew Alistair would pull himself out of it eventually, and she found her own peace in helping him. They spoke about Rebecca often, cried when they felt the need, and laughed when they remembered the good times.

"Laila? Come to Europe with us this summer," Sterling whispered in her ear. "Please?" His parents had bought the twins round trip tickets to Europe and accommodations in the best hotels across the continent. Sterling had suggested the idea and Alistair had practically begged for her to join them.

"Yes," she finally said. "I'd love to go with you." Her parents had finally relented and agreed to let her take the trip. She thought they preferred her traveling with two strong boys to a group of teenage girls.

"Good, because I've already bought your plane ticket," he grinned down at her.

"You didn't have to do that," she smiled.

"Just consider it a graduation present."

Laila's hand caressed the diamond encrusted pendant which rested against her chest. Sterling had given it to her last night after they had made love for hours. Sterling had promised her that they would be together forever. Laila believed it, too. She believed it with all her heart. "I love you, Sterling," she whispered and gave him a sweet kiss.

A knock came from the door. "It must be my parents!" Laila whispered in panic. Sterling froze, not sure of what to do. Laila acted quickly, pushing him off and searching quickly for her clothes. They heard the knock again and it snapped Sterling out of his trance. "Shit," he swore quietly as he searched the sheets for his boxers.

"Laila, darling, are you in there?" came a nasally, high pitched voice. The couple burst into laughter. Laila finished pulling her sundress over her head and chuckling, walked over and opened the door.

"You are such a jerk!" She playfully pushed Alistair as he walked into the room. He wore a royal blue cap and gown, his eyes brighter than she had seen them in months.

"You're supposed to be graduating today, not fornicating!" He kissed Laila quickly on the cheek. "You should get dressed, little brother, unless you're planning on walking in nothing but your boxers."

Sterling shot Alistair a death glare as he bent over and pulled up his pants. Alistair chuckled and turned back to her. "So, are you coming with us?"

Laila nodded. "Yes," she answered.

"Thank you," Alistair said softly. "It means a lot; but you know that."

Laila reached for his hand and squeezed it tightly. "You're welcome. But why are you thanking me? You two are taking me to Europe, I should be thanking you."

"You can thank us later," Sterling smiled at her, pulling his shirt over his head. "We're going to be late for graduation."

Laila giggled in excitement and grabbed her robes from the back of her chair. Alistair handed Sterling his cap and gown.

The three of them ran out of the room and down the hallway into the warm summer air.

CHAPTER FORTY-FIVE

"**W**ell, here we are." Tennille stared out at the graduating class seated in front of her. Tate sat in the front row, looking proud. The Pierce twins, who had been arguing over something, quickly stopped and turned their attention toward her. Laila couldn't wipe the smile from her face, practically bouncing out of her chair. She could see the back of Chase's head as he leaned forward in his seat, most likely passed out or trying to convince himself he was sober enough to graduate.

"As valedictorian, I'm supposed to give an inspirational speech about the future, use metaphors and tell you to always remember your time at Harper's. But I don't know anything about the future and I'm not really feeling inspirational at the moment. The truth is, I shouldn't be giving this speech right now. If it were my choice, I would be sitting in the audience with the rest of you."

A murmur rose from the crowd. Some students shifted in their seats, while parents craned their necks towards the stage, unsure if they had heard her correctly.

"I've been asked not to say their names. I've been asked not to mention the events that happened earlier this year. But we are all thinking about them, as we should be. They were part of this school, part of our lives, and part of our experience at Harper's Preparatory."

She glanced quickly at the faculty to her right. Headmaster Bradley glared at her and the other teachers either looked embarrassed or shocked.

"Randal Showman, your true valedictorian, Rebecca Valencourt, Kalyn Andretti. They were our best friends, classmates, acquaintances; they were someone's children, someone's brother and sisters. You may not have known them but, for some of us, we are still struggling to mend the pieces of our hearts that broke when they died."

Tennille stared directly at Laila who sniffled and wiped away a tear. Tennille smiled and gave her a quick wink.

"I've learned something from the death of my best friend. I've learned that as strong as you think you may be, there is always something that can break you. But once you're broken, lying in a million pieces on the ground, the getting back up is what truly defines you as a person, what truly shows your strength. I hope, with all my heart, that your time at Harper's has given you the tools you need to pull yourself off the ground because, inevitably, we will all be there — the metaphorical gun to our head and razor at our wrist."

She heard gasps from the crowd.

"Please, look back at your time here with a wise eye. Look back and recognize that you've been given a gift, a privilege that other people don't have. You have survived when others have not. You have experienced the worst that life has to offer. And you have risen above it. Don't try to forget what happened here. Learn from it, use it. Because if they are remembered, then their deaths may not be as senseless as they seem."

Tennille scanned the crowd again. Tears and sniffles interrupted the quiet.

"I'm sorry if this isn't what you expected. I'm sorry if I've put a damper on your graduation day. But it needed to be said; they needed to be remembered. They wouldn't want us to be sad for them. They would want us to enjoy ourselves. Guys, we're getting out of here! We're gaining responsibility, shedding our childhood, throwing ourselves into the unknown. As scary as that sounds, I know all of us are ready for it. We will shape our future and the futures of those around us with the knowledge and experiences we have had at Harper's. And, if I know my graduating class like I think I do, not one moment of our futures will be dull; not one moment will be without hope or good intention. So congratulations to all of us. This moment belongs to us. We deserve it. We've earned it. And we'll share it with the three who couldn't be here today because they are as much a part of our future as they are our past."

Silence lingered across the broad, green lawn for a few long seconds. Laila stood and began to clap. Sterling and Alistair followed, and one by one, the rest of the class rose and applauded. Tennille walked back to her seat next to the headmaster.

***

Laila waited for her name to be called and eventually received a handshake and a diploma. After four years of high school, and one crazy year at Harper's, the official act took but a second. Such a small existence, she thought to herself. They all had no idea what lay ahead in the real world. But that was part of growing up. That was part of becoming who you were meant to be. She found her parents in the audience. Proud tears of joy streaked her mother's cheeks and her father smiled up at her with love and pride.

She took her seat and waited impatiently for the headmaster to finish the ceremony. Standing up with the rest of the class, she moved her tassels across her cap, hearing a slow yet audible excitement starting to rumble through the seats. And then it was over — one hundred and seventeen royal blue caps flew through the air as cheers of joy and perfect happiness filled the grounds.

Welcome to the rest of your life.

ABOUT THE AUTHOR

Lydia Kelly is the author of *Screaming in the Silence*,
published in 2010 by WorldMaker Media. She was
born and raised in Oregon where she currently lives
with her husband and son. A Harper's Education is
the first in a series of novels for young adults.

HARPER'S

PREPARATORY

MASSACHUSETTS

CONSCIENTIA